'You…wanted to talk about the meeting…' Amy said breathlessly.

But before she could carry on Rocco's long fingers had started doing things to her body, just as his lips had done when he had kissed her that time, except now it seemed different, because this was happening slowly.

'In time,' Rocco said softly. His hand pulled her towards him and his lips met hers with an intensity that had been building up for days.

'Rocco…'

'Shh. Don't talk. You want this. We both do.'

Amy sighed. This wasn't the sort of man she had ever imagined herself being drawn to. Security was what she needed. Rocco Losi wasn't secure, and he didn't follow the rules of the game as she knew it. He was a predator who saw what he wanted and took it.

Cathy Williams is originally from Trinidad but has lived in England for a number of years. She currently has a house in Warwickshire, which she shares with her husband Richard, her three daughters, Charlotte, Olivia and Emma, and their pet cat Salem. She adores writing romantic fiction and would love one of her girls to become a writer—although at the moment she is happy enough if they do their homework and agree not to bicker with one another.

Recent titles by the same author:
Modern Romance™

THE MILLIONAIRE'S REVENGE
RICCARDO'S SECRET CHILD
THE RICH MAN'S MISTRESS
THE GREEK TYCOON'S SECRET CHILD
HIS VIRGIN SECRETARY

THE ITALIAN TYCOON'S MISTRESS

BY
CATHY WILLIAMS

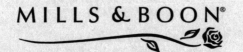

MILLS & BOON®

All the characters in this book have no existence outside the imagination of the author, and have no relation whatsoever to anyone bearing the same name or names. They are not even distantly inspired by any individual known or unknown to the author, and all the incidents are pure invention.

*First published in Great Britain 2004
Harlequin Mills & Boon Limited,
Eton House, 18-24 Paradise Road, Richmond, Surrey TW9 1SR*

© Cathy Williams 2004

ISBN 0 263 83763 7

*Set in Times Roman 10½ on 12 pt.
01-0804-51562*

*Printed and bound in Spain
by Litografia Rosés, S.A., Barcelona*

CHAPTER ONE

'WHAT'S this?'

It wasn't so much of a question as a demand for an immediate explanation. The past two days had been regularly punctuated by such demands, thinly veiled as polite enquiries. Rocco Losi had descended into the cosy feather bed of Losi Construction like a panther leaping into a gathering of easy prey, intent on a kill.

Richard Newton glanced worriedly to where one long brown finger was pointing at a small entry on the printout and sighed.

'That's one of the subsids,' he explained, leaning forward to peer at the entry and then subsiding back into his chair with a feeling of doom.

'One of the subsids. Where's the paperwork relating to this particular *subsid*?' Rocco pushed his chair back and coolly contemplated the fair-haired man who seemed to be caught in a state of nervous agitation.

This exercise was proving to be a nightmare from hell and, as far as Rocco was concerned, the level of the executives only helped to aid and abet the impression. It was a marvel that his father's company managed to make the profits it did considering that a great majority of the chief executives were of the old-fashioned, jocular, verging-on-retirement type. Richard Newton, the accounts manager now perspiring in front of him, was one of the younger members of management and Rocco would hardly have called him cutting edge. In fact, the man wouldn't have lasted more than five seconds in his own corporate giant where dead wood was shed and under-performers were left in no doubt of their eventual fate, should change not be forthcoming.

But then the cut and thrust of life in New York's fast lane was considerably more savage than here, in Shakespeare's County.

Rocco placed his hands flatly on the surface of his father's desk and enunciated his next few words with grim, measured brutality.

'Listen to me very carefully, Mr Newton. I don't want to be here. I have been compelled to leave my offices in New York because of events which have left me no choice. However, I am here now and I don't intend to give you all a perfunctory pat on the back and leave you to muddle along the way you appear to have always muddled along. I do not expect to have to ask any questions because I expect all the information I require on my father's company to be right here. In this room. Sitting on this desk. Waiting for me to look at. Do I make myself absolutely clear?'

Rocco Losi watched the man sitting opposite him nod weakly and felt not a scrap of compassion. He wasn't here to get a popularity award or to make friends. He was here to temporarily take charge of his father's company so that public confidence in it could be maintained until such time as he could depart these shores back to the city that had been his home for over ten years.

Nor was he prepared to do a surface job. That wasn't his style. He had come, albeit against his will, and he intended to turn over whatever stones were necessary to make sure that Losi Construction was performing to its highest possible level.

The file had been fetched and placed in front of him. Without bothering to look at him, Rocco informed

Richard Newton that he was to remain precisely where he was until he had answered all questions to his personal satisfaction.

He took his time with the file, barely aware of the man patiently waiting for him to finish, then he sat back and looked at Richard Newton in silence for a few seconds.

'Explain to me where this particular subsidiary fits in with the general profit-making scheme of the company.' He linked his fingers casually together and waited. He had always felt that people, generally, underestimated the great virtue of silence. In his experience, there was nothing more persuasive when it came to getting a truthful answer than silence. It could be unnerving and quite deadly.

'Ah. Yes, well…your father makes a healthy profit with his company. It's one of the most respected building firms in the area, you know. And with the boom in housing over the years, with no end in sight, well, as you can see from the general spreadsheets, things are doing quite nicely. More than quite nicely.'

Rocco watched this inexpert evasion of his question with hooded eyes. Nor did he encourage the meandering by saying a word. Instead, he glanced at his watch, then returned his attention to Richard Newton's flushed face.

'As for where it fits in with the profit-making…well…it doesn't. Not really. You probably don't understand how things work out here, Mr Losi. I mean, you're accustomed to a more aggressive type of environment, I guess…'

'I'm looking for an answer in one sentence, Mr Newton. You are the chief accountant. Surely it cannot be that difficult.'

'This particular subsidiary is the goodwill arm of the firm, so to speak. Amy Hogan looks after it. You could say that she handles the equivalent of legal pro bono work. Your father was, *is*, very keen on the idea of giving back. Of course, Amy does handle profit-making work as well…'

Rocco frowned. 'I thought I had met all the relevant personnel. The name rings no bells.'

'That's because she doesn't exactly work in this building. She has an office closer to Birmingham because she's on the move a lot of the time, overseeing things in the city centre.'

'What is her position in the company?'

'She's…well, one of the executives…'

'I believe I asked to interview all the executives.'

'Ah. Yes. You did. But she couldn't make it in yesterday…'

'Because…?' Rocco's voice was ominous in its smoothness. 'Severe ill health, perhaps? Or was she out of the country?'

For a few seconds, Richard Newton seriously debated going for the severe ill health option. 'She said she was busy.'

'She. Said. She. Was. Busy.' Rocco was finding it a little difficult to believe his ears. He had made his orders perfectly clear from the very first moment he had stepped foot in the company. He was so accustomed to having his orders obeyed without question, and usually at the speed of light, that the idea of someone casually ignoring them because *she was busy* was very nearly beyond the realm of his understanding.

'Amy hardly ever stops!' Richard elaborated in a desperate attempt to avert the equivalent of a missile homing in ruthlessly onto its target, judging from the expression on Rocco's face. 'And right now she's working on a particularly big project…'

'Would that be a particularly big *non-profit-making* project, by any chance?'

'Community centre on a sink estate in the city centre,' was the mumbled response.

Rocco felt his tightly reined-in patience begin to unravel. This was a highly unusual occurrence. In that rarefied place that he inhabited, where power and influence afforded him the luxury of utter self-assurance, stumbling blocks were things that he tackled with utmost cool. Hitches in multimillion-dollar deals did not rouse his impatience, merely his professional curiosity and intellectual interest. They cropped up occasionally and more often than not he simply sorted them out with his usual unerring precision.

The thought of some minor middle-management woman deliberately choosing to ignore his summons because she basically couldn't be bothered made him grit his teeth together in rising rage.

He leaned forward, elbows on the desk. 'Here is a little job for you, Mr Newton. You telephone Miss Hogan as soon as you walk out of this office and inform her that I will be paying her a little visit this afternoon. I will expect her to be waiting for me in her office, *however busy she is*, at precisely three o'clock. If she is not there, feel free to assure her that her head will most definitely be on the block.'

Richard Newton opened his mouth to state that dismissals of executives were taken to the board of directors, and closed his mouth before he could utter a word. This man did not play by the usual rules. He was a law unto himself and the gentlemanly codes of behaviour that had operated within the hallowed walls of Losi Construction would be brushed aside as minor irritations. He nodded and exited the room with a feeling of deep relief, leaving

Rocco to broodingly ponder yet something else to deal with that he had not foreseen.

If he and his father had had any sort of ongoing communication between them, he would have arrived here with some expectation of what he was going to find. As it was, the feud that had driven him to make his fortune on the other side of the Atlantic meant that he had arrived in England with no knowledge of how his father's company operated or even whether it was successful or not.

He raked his fingers through his hair and buzzed his secretary in to arrange a driver to take him to wherever the Hogan woman's office was in the city centre. Then he proceeded to spend the remainder of the morning going through profit-and-loss columns, summoning up information on the computer, while maintaining contact with his own offices across the Atlantic via his own laptop computer.

He only broke off at two when he was interrupted by his secretary informing him that his driver was ready.

He didn't know what he had expected to find. Losi Construction was located on the outskirts of Stratford and was housed in an old period building that reeked of Old World elegance. It was as far removed from his own super-modern, innovative glass building in the heart of New York as chalk was from cheese.

At the back of his mind, he expected to find an office on a similar but smaller scale. Something Victorian, perhaps, with the high ceilings and understated elegance that he remembered from way back.

He was slightly taken aback when, after a slow drive out of the country into the myriad cluttered streets of the city, the driver finally pulled up outside something small, concrete and tacked onto a newsagent's in a parade of fairly disreputable-looking shops.

'Are you sure you have got the right place?' Rocco eyed the dodgy front with a frown. A little gang of youths was loitering in front of the off-licence, obviously having nothing better to do on a brilliant summer day than hang out in a threatening fashion.

'Of course, sir. I have often come to fetch Miss Hogan when her car is out of action.'

'A frequent occurrence, is it?'

'She's very fond of that little Mini,' Edward said neutrally, 'even though it plays up from time to time.'

Rocco grunted, barely hearing this piece of uninvited information. He pushed open the car door and slung his long, powerful body out, then he leant down to prop himself against the window. 'I will call you when I'm ready to be collected.'

'Yes, sir.'

Which, Rocco figured, would be in under an hour. He had no intention of going over any books with the woman. That could be done in the comfort of his father's office. No. He would simply prepare her for the possibility that all this community housing rubbish would come to a swift end should his father be unable to return to active work, leaving Rocco to take over to his satisfaction before he departed for New York. If the company wanted to donate to charitable causes, there were ways and means of doing just that, which would additionally bring in tax relief on the donations. Time, energy and manpower were to be spent on the profitable side of the business. Losi Construction was not an unofficial branch of the Samaritans.

With that objective firmly in his mind, Rocco pushed open the door to the office and stepped into a world he had not visited for a very long time indeed. The world of cheap furniture, threadbare carpets and seeming chaos.

There was no reception area. Five desks were crammed into a room roughly half the size of his own office in New York and one entire wall was dominated by an intricate map of a housing estate, from an aerial view. Grimy windows had been flung open to allow some fresh air in and an overhead fan threatened to wreak havoc on any paperwork that wasn't securely weighted down.

In this alarmingly basic atmosphere work was, however, going on, although it immediately stopped the minute he walked in, with five pairs of eyes focusing on him with unconcealed interest. Three men and two women, all in their twenties. Two of the men wore their hair scraped back into ponytails and conversely the women had short cropped hairdos.

'I am looking for an Amy Hogan,' Rocco said, moving forward so that several more details in the room sprang into unfortunate prominence. Such as the notice-board propped against the wall at the back, with messages tacked over every square centimetre of its surface, the wire bins most of which were full, and a box of tools whose purpose he could only guess at.

'In the back.' One of the lads stepped forward and eyed Rocco suspiciously, putting out one hand when Rocco tried to head in the mentioned direction. 'Whoa! Where do you think you're going, mate?'

'I am here to see Miss Hogan.'

'And you are…?'

'Rocco Losi.'

The hand dropped and there was a heightened sense of interest now.

'I have an appointment with Miss Hogan, in case she hasn't mentioned it.'

'Nope. She hasn't. How's your dad doing? Name's Freddy, by the way, mate. Soz about the lack of welcome mate, but you can't be too careful in these parts.' Freddy held out his hand, which was surprisingly firm when Rocco shook it.

'Off-licence was broken into a fortnight ago,' one of the cropped-haired women interjected. 'Three men just broke through the plate glass and hauled as much as they could, as cool as you like, never mind the alarm bells.'

'Took the coppers a good ten minutes to get here...'

'By which time, they'd scarpered...'

'Old Mr Singh was pretty shaken up about it...'

'I see you've met my staff.' The voice was low, husky and threaded with amusement. Rocco looked up to see a woman standing in the doorway, dressed in the same casual style as everyone else seemed to be: jeans and a stripy teeshirt, with a pair of trainers. 'I'm Amy Hogan and you must be Antonio's son.'

The softening in her voice when she mentioned his father's name stirred something inside him and Rocco met her open smile with a gritted one of his own. Five feet four, if that, straight brown hair, wide-spaced brown eyes, sprinkling of freckles across the bridge of a short, straight nose.

What, he wondered, had possessed his father to employ someone who looked so young to handle sums of money that a good many would baulk at? To fling about at her own discretion? A community centre here, a refuge there, a park somewhere else...?

He hadn't actually seen her CV, but now that he had laid eyes on her he decided that he'd better check her credentials.

'Perhaps we could go somewhere private for a talk,' Rocco said, moving towards her.

'My office is just at the back.' God, he was tall. Amy could feel herself craning up to look at him. Tall and so incredibly good-looking that she had to wrench her eyes away or risk staring shamelessly. He was olive-skinned, with black hair and eyes so piercingly blue that even when she had looked past him she could still feel them boring into her.

Richard hadn't told her what he looked like. She wished she had asked, so that she wouldn't now be standing here, gaping.

Fortunately, he had told her everything else about him, paying particular attention to his arrogance, not that she could have missed it. It was stamped all over him like a handprint.

She plastered her brightest smile on her face. 'Would you like something to drink? Tea? Coffee? Actually, scrap the coffee. We ran out a couple of days ago and no one's got around to replacing it. So that's tea or water.'

'I'm fine. I'm just here for a little…chat…and then I will be on my way.'

Amy shrugged and led the way to her office, which was just another room, smaller than the first but in a similarly worn state. However, it did contain a desk, behind which she moved to sit, and a couple of chairs, one of which she indicated to Rocco.

He seemed to dwarf the room. It was an illusion, of course, but it was still unsettling. Something about the unhurried way he looked around him before finally settling his attention on her rattled her. Surprising because, in the sort of work she did, she came into contact with men who were really a lot more unsettling than Rocco Losi.

'What can I do for you?' Amy asked, smilingly polite although the smile was in danger of wearing a bit thin.

'I believe I asked to see you at my father's offices yesterday?'

'I know. Sorry about that but I was really very busy and I just couldn't find the time to get away. How is your father doing? We were all really worried when he was taken ill with pneumonia. He told me that he was just a little run-down. It was a complete shock to learn that he'd been taken into hospital. I've tried to get in to see him every day, but he was still so weak that I don't think my presence there did much good at all.'

'Let us get one thing straight, Miss Hogan. I am here for absolutely the least amount of time possible. In the time that I am here, I expect cooperation from every member of my father's staff. That includes yourself, however distant your outpost appears to be.'

Amy stopped smiling and met his stare with one of her own. 'Please accept my apologies. Now, perhaps you would like to tell me what I can do for you.' Richard had been vague but ominous on the matter of Rocco's visit and she hadn't pressed him, assuming that he just wanted a quick run-down of the projects they had recently worked on and were currently undertaking. She was becoming uneasily aware that her blithe optimism might have been a tad misplaced.

'What you can do for me is to tell me what your credentials are.'

'I beg your pardon?'

'Your credentials.'

'Is that really necessary?' she asked, flushing under the cold, unwavering stare. 'Antonio has always trusted me...'

'My father is not running this company at the moment. I am. As things stand, there is a chance he may not be sufficiently fit to return to work, in which case it is my duty to take the company in hand and get it running the way I see fit before I leave this country.' Despite the whirring of a fan that was poised perilously on top of one of the gun-metal-grey filing cabinets, the room was like an oven and Rocco pushed up the sleeves of his shirt. How these people could work in here was beyond him. His first summer in New York, before he had begun his meteoric rise, had been spent in a box like this. One bedroom, a tiny bathroom, a kitchen and the heat pouring through inadequate windows like treacle. Ten years on, his memories of such discomfort were blessedly dim. Now, his apartment was plush, air-conditioned throughout to cope with the soaring temperatures in summer, and a testimony to what top designers could do when money was no object.

'What does that have to do with my credentials, Mr Losi?' Amy asked coolly.

On the verge of snapping, Rocco leaned forward and subjected her to the full force of his overpowering personality. 'To be blunt, Miss Hogan, I'll tell you what I have found since coming here. I have found a company that is successful more through default than strategy. The construction business is booming and my father happens to have cornered the market simply because Losi Construction has been around for a very long time and has consequently benefited from its reputation. The directors seem content to sit around and accept this happy state of affairs without questioning the possibility that other, more aggressive firms might creep up to challenge their monopoly of the market. It doesn't take a financial wizard to spot the flaws in this way of thinking. Added to this, I find substantial sums of money being flung in the direction of a kid so that she can play at being a charity worker.'

'A *kid? Playing at being a charity worker?* Would you be talking about *me*, Mr Losi?'

'Very perceptive.' Rocco lounged back in his chair and looked at her with cool indifference. Her brain seemed sharp enough but she was still a kid of, what…nineteen? Twenty? No make-up whatsoever. He was accustomed to dealing with women in business and was similarly accustomed to the power suits and the face paint.

'I happen to be twenty-six years old, not that it's any of your business…'

'Oh, but that's where you are wrong. It is my business. At least at this point in time. I am now your boss and, as your boss, I would be very interested in knowing what experience you have that qualifies you to deal with the sums of money you have been dealing with. Who is your immediate boss?'

'My immediate boss has always been your father!'

'So you're telling me that you have free rein to do whatever you like, build whatever bijou shelters for the homeless that you want and what…? Casually mention it to my father? Run it by him at the odd meeting when you can find the time?'

Amy felt a rush of angry blood to her head. This was beyond arrogance, but she was caught between a rock and a hard place. There was no way that she could throw him out of her office because he was, as he had made sure to point out, her boss for the time being and, more chillingly, might well be her boss for rather longer if Antonio somehow found himself having to take early retirement. Antonio was now in his seventies and the doctor had told her that the pneumonia might be far more debilitating at his age than it would have been had he been younger, especially when his angina was taken into consideration.

'I resent your implication that this outfit lacks professionalism!'

'Now why on earth would I be tempted to imply that?'

Rocco looked around him pointedly. At the grimy walls of the office, the tattered carpet, the cheap bookshelves groaning under the weight of law and land management books.

'You, Mr Losi, are an extremely offensive person,' Amy said through gritted teeth and was rewarded with a thunderous frown.

'I will choose to ignore that observation.'

'And, furthermore, the state of my office has nothing to do with the quality of my work! Or maybe things work differently in New York?'

Rocco could hardly believe his ears. *Just who did this pipsqueak think she was?* The brown almond-shaped eyes were glittering with anger and it took some effort to call upon his formidable self-control. That, in itself, was a novel experience.

'I think we're getting off the point here, Miss Hogan.' His voice was cold and measured. 'In order of priority, I want to see your credentials, look in detail at this project you are working on and have a run-down of the cost. Additionally, I want to have a report from you on my desk by tomorrow morning, covering all the money that has been spent over the past two years on non-profit-making schemes and the few you have done that have actually benefited the company.'

Amy gaped and then laughed out loud. 'I'm afraid that just won't be possible.'

'Sorry. I don't believe I just heard that.'

'There's no way I can do all that in time for tomorrow morning. Richard should have all that information anyway. Now, was there anything else?' Okay, so she was reacting, allowing the man to get to her, but she couldn't help herself. She stood up and stretched out her hand in dismissal. Rocco looked at the outstretched hand coolly and didn't budge.

'Sit back down, Miss Hogan. I'm not nearly through with you.'

'I could have that information to you by the end of the week,' she said, resuming her seat and looking with deep loathing at the man calmly sitting opposite her.

'You say you're twenty-six.' Rocco crossed his legs and ignored the olive branch she had extended. His allotted time to be spent here had come and gone and he realised that he was rather enjoying this clash of intellect and personality. To his mild surprise. 'Which means you've been working for Losi Construction for what…? Four years…? You must have certainly made your presence felt quite strongly in a short space of time to have warranted the heady climb you've enjoyed.'

'Ten years,' Amy admitted grudgingly.

'Ten years? That doesn't add up.'

'Doesn't add up to what?'

'To you leaving university.'

The silence stretched interminably. 'I didn't go to university, Mr Losi. I joined your father's firm straight from school.'

Rocco couldn't have looked more stunned if she had announced that she had been raised by a pack of wolves in Africa.

'Not everyone gets the chance to go to university!' Amy snapped defensively. 'It's a privilege, not a right.' She couldn't withstand the direct look in those piercing blue eyes and she lowered hers so that she could stare at the tip of a letter propped up on the desk.

'You mean your grades were insufficient to get you into sixth form?'

'I mean, Mr Losi—' she drew in a deep breath and shot

him a quick glance from under her lashes '—that my mother died when I was young and I was brought up single-handedly by my father. He developed Alzheimer's when I was fourteen, and by the time I was sixteen I had no choice but to let the social services find somewhere for him to live. I finished my exams but I couldn't continue my studies. I got a job working with your father and was lucky enough to be able to stay with a foster family until I was old enough to move out and find somewhere to rent. I would have loved to have been able to continue on at school and to have gone to university, but I could barely manage with Dad at home. I didn't have a choice.' She fiddled with the pen on her desk, knowing that he was staring at her. This was his big chance now, she thought bitterly. She had no credentials, no degree in a useful subject.

'Right. So your credentials rest entirely on experience.'

'As a clerk. Then as your father's assistant. We worked together to build up a scheme to help the community and eventually I was given responsibility for managing it on my own.'

'I see.' Rocco felt himself grapple in unfamiliar territory. 'And where…is your father now?'

'He died two years ago.' It would never stop hurting to talk about it, which was why she never did. 'It was a blessing. He was very confused towards the end. He couldn't remember who I was, kept getting me mixed up with Mum. So. There you have it.' He had dragged this out of her and she hated him for it. 'Would you like me to have this all typed up and on your desk as well? My life history?'

Rocco flushed darkly. 'There is no need for sarcasm.'

'Oh, was I being sarcastic?' She clung with relief to

her need to attack. 'I thought I was just obeying your instructions.'

'My father trusted you and naturally I will give you credit for that trust.' He shrugged and leaned forward, elbows resting on his knees. 'However sympathetic I am towards the hardships that propelled you out of school prematurely and into the working environment, that does not mean that the sums of money being spent on charitable causes should remain unchecked. I am here to run a business and the first rule of business is that a company survives only if it makes money.'

'I realise that,' Amy said impatiently.

'Do you?' He sat back, once again comfortable with his persona. He had left England with nothing and climbed his way up solely on his own abilities. The value of making money had been embedded in him from the first moment he had begun working and living in New York.

'Of course I do!'

'In which case you will not mind me inspecting every penny that has been spent by your little outfit over the past two years.'

'The information will be with you by the end of the week.' And Lord only knew how he was going to react to the figures. He thought in black and white. No profit, no use. The concept of not making profit for the sake of returning to the community would be lost on him.

'I don't want it on my desk,' Rocco said slowly.

'But…'

'I want you to bring it to me. Hand deliver the bad news, so to speak. That way we can go through it all together and you will be able to better understand why I intend to bring your cosy little office here to an end should I find myself having to linger here longer than I anticipate.' He stood up, noticing that her face had drained of colour, and impatiently told himself that he was first and foremost a businessman. And not just any businessman. His shrewdness was legendary. How shrewd would he be if he allowed an unreasonable tug of compassion to undermine his ability to run a company?

'Your father would never stand for it,' Amy said confidently.

'My father is in hospital, Miss Hogan, and the running of this company is entirely entrusted to me.'

'Which is ludicrous, considering…'

'Considering…what?' Cold blue eyes narrowed threateningly. He stood up, all six feet two of dominant alpha male, and stared at her, waiting for an answer to a remark Amy knew she should never have made in the first place.

'Considering…this is probably small potatoes to you,' she improvised rapidly. 'A bit dull, I imagine. You must do things differently over in New York and you might want to consider that when you start making your decisions.' Considering, she thought to herself, that you've seen your father the grand total of four times in a decade. She knew that because Antonio had told her, because he had sheltered her under his wing and she had somehow become the child he had never really had.

'Thank you so much for your advice,' Rocco drawled, flicking on his mobile so that he could tell his driver to come for him. He tucked it into the pocket of his shirt and smiled coolly at her. 'Though I rarely follow advice. I have usually found that it tends to be loaded and not necessarily in my favour.' She looked down but he could feel her stewing, itching to fling him some caustic remark, and the enjoyment he had felt earlier kicked in him again.

'Friday,' he told her. 'At my office. Bring the books and everything to do with whatever you're working on at the moment and whatever you may happen to have in the pipeline. I'll be waiting for you at three-thirty.'

Outside, the gang of teenage youths had dispersed, replaced by two girls with pushchairs who were chatting. They looked young enough to be at school. Around him, the scenery consisted of cluttered streets leading off the main road. Edward was there, waiting. He must have just gone around the corner for a cup of tea until Rocco called him.

Rocco didn't immediately go to the car. He stood and carried on his leisurely inspection of the area, then he looked behind him to the office.

Nightmare though it was to be thrown into this situation, when he himself had his own extensive businesses to run, he had to admit that at least it wasn't going to be boring.

They might all be scuttling around right now, whispering about him behind his back, but they would be very happy when he dragged the company into the twenty-first century and quadrupled the profits, which he was pretty certain he could do without a great deal of effort.

That was one of the most disillusioning things about life, he thought grimly. Money always ended up talking...

CHAPTER TWO

AMY made sure that she was at the headquarters well before the appointed time of three-thirty. She had had three days to consider the threat that Rocco's presence posed and several missed hours of sleep to work out that the best way of dealing with the man was to creep around him as much as she was capable of doing. Shooting her mouth off and turning up late for their meeting through some misplaced urge to prove a point would bring his wrath hurtling down on her like a ton of bricks.

It didn't help that she had been to see Antonio the day before, to find that the cocktail of antibiotics being fed into him was not working as efficiently as they had expected. He certainly couldn't be asked pivotal questions regarding the company. In fact, he dozed on and off for the duration of her visit and she was rewarded, on the way out, by the depressing news from the consultant that Antonio would certainly remain in hospital for at least another three weeks, after which he would benefit from a recuperative break in Italy where his relatives could look after him and where the concerns of his business would not intrude on his recovery. Rocco had been making all the necessary phone calls to get things moving in that direction.

Which left a worst-case scenario, as far as Amy was concerned.

Rocco would take over and begin making his changes, and change one would be to exterminate her and her fellow members of staff.

24

Depressingly, the only person she felt she could possibly discuss this with was Antonio, who was not available for comment. Antonio had always been the first person she turned to with a problem, the only shoulder she had really ever cried on, and having him out of reach was a severe blow.

She half expected Rocco to keep her waiting, having read somewhere that this was an age-old ploy for establishing superiority, but she was shown directly into his office to find him sitting behind his father's desk with a stack of files in front of him that looked depressingly familiar.

His face was unsmiling and as coldly handsome as she remembered. A face that would drive any portrait painter into the throes of excitement, with its perfect bone structure and harshly beautiful lines, but one that just filled her with dislike. She found his stunning eyes hard and forbidding and his emotional detachment radiated around him like a dangerous force field. It was difficult to maintain her self-composure when faced with this and when he nodded to the chair facing him, she sunk into it with relief.

'You're on time,' he drawled, leaning back in the chair. 'Amazing. I gather from your colleagues here that your timetables don't often dovetail with everyone else's.'

Amy ventured a polite smile. 'It's difficult when you're working out in the field, Mr Losi. Sometimes, things have a tendency to overrun and, with the long drive out to Stratford, I can get behind schedule with meetings. I've brought the files you wanted.' She reached down to her briefcase, snapped it open and extracted a clear window envelope bulging with various project notes.

Instead of reaching over for them, Rocco didn't move a muscle.

'Bad news for you, I'm afraid, Miss Hogan.' He tapped softly on the arm of his chair with one finger and continued looking at her with those incredible, shuttered blue eyes. 'Although I suspect you already know what's coming if you have been to visit my father.'

'I think it's excellent news if you're talking about the doctor's suggestion that he go to Italy to recuperate.' Keep it upbeat, she thought. Don't let him register any trepidation because Rocco Losi would be onto it like a shark scenting blood. Of course, he could do as he liked and no doubt would, but she wouldn't give up without a fight and she certainly wouldn't abandon her dignity in the process. 'You have no idea how hard he's been working over the past couple of years. He's due for a rest, even if it's not exactly in circumstances he could have foreseen.'

'There was no necessity for him to be working flat out,' Rocco said, not bothering to pull any punches. 'Not if he had had members of staff on whom he could rely.'

'I'm not about to be drawn on criticising anyone in this company,' Amy told him. 'Perhaps we should get down to the business of going through my files?' Belatedly, she wondered whether she should have been a little less terse. Rocco Losi would have spent most of his adult life in a position of rising power, being fawned upon by people in the expectation that they might get something out of him. Men like him would be used to displays of subservience and would be conditioned to expect it. Putting him in his place wasn't going to get her far, but then there was just so much ingratiating she was prepared to do. Criticising people who had supported her in the past was out of the question.

'Oh, I have already had a preliminary look at some of the figures,' Rocco said lazily. He sat forward and placed both elbows on the desk. 'The last little project you did was cheap at a little over fifty thousand pounds, compared to the rest of your schemes…'

'But only a small percentage of the total earnings of Losi Construction,' Amy pointed out, stilling the nervous pounding inside her. 'It was always agreed…'

'I am so glad you used the past tense. Let me put you in the picture, Miss Hogan. I will be here for the next six months. Even when my father has fully recovered, it's been recommended that he does not return to work full time. He will, naturally, remain in overall charge, but in name only. I will ensure that the company is running the way I want it to be before I go, in the capable hands of whomever I judge to be up to the job.'

'Six months?' Amy said weakly.

'At least.'

'Don't you have other things to do? What about your company in New York? Shouldn't you be rushing back there?'

'Unlike this organisation, I can easily maintain links with my business concerns in America. I have people in place who are geared to assume responsibility in my absence. And there are such things as airplanes that can deliver me to America within hours if I need to be there.'

'How very efficient.'

Rocco's dark brows met in a frown. 'Efficiency is the basis of a successful operation. Which brings me neatly to you.' He relaxed back in his chair and proceeded to look at her very carefully.

'I am extremely efficient at what I do.'

'That's as may be, but your level of efficiency isn't really the crux of the matter here, is it? You're supremely efficient at what you do. It's simply that what you do brings no money into the company.'

'There's more to life than just making money.' Two

bright patches of angry colour had appeared on her cheeks and she found that she was leaning forward, her hands balled into fists. 'I personally find it very sad when someone's only focus in life is creating wealth. What do you do with all your money, Mr Losi? Stick it into bank accounts and then spend jolly evenings poring over your statements and patting yourself on the back at what a clever boy you've been?'

Rocco looked at the earnest face glaring stubbornly at him and felt it again. That sudden rush of invigoration. It was like tasting something powerfully addictive that he hadn't tasted in a long time, not since he'd been building up his career, when the doubts had been balanced equally with the self-assurance. Success had become an assumption for him and successful men, he had discovered, invariably became surrounded by like-minded individuals, people whose sights were firmly set in the same direction. No one contradicted him because his vast power and influence rendered him virtually untouchable.

'Oh, I can think of infinitely more interesting ways of spending an evening,' he drawled, perversely enjoying the delicate flush that invaded her face as she cottoned on to the exact meaning of what he had said.

The sexual innuendo, leaping out of nowhere, crashed into Amy like a runaway freight train. For a few seconds her imagination took dangerous flight and painted pictures that she had to force herself to push away. He really was a stunningly attractive male, she conceded shakily. That black hair and those thick, luxuriant dark lashes that could droop to conceal his fabulous eyes, that wide, sexy mouth. She blinked and sat up a little straighter.

'What do you intend to do, Mr Losi?' She firmly brought the conversation back to business. 'I have a staff of five very dedicated people, all of whom are one hun-

dred per cent committed to what we do. Two of them are
married and need the salary they earn. Well, we all do,
come to that. I'm also in mid-project at the moment. It's
not just a question of me.'

'Therefore…what?'

'This is hopeless. I can't see the point of being here.'
Amy stood up but then found that she was hovering.

'Rule one in business is to never let your emotions
control your responses. Sit back down.' Rocco stood up
and began prowling through the office, hands firmly stuck
in his trouser pockets, forcing Amy to twist around to
follow his progress. He paused in front of the generous,
old-fashioned bookshelf and perched on the protruding
ledge that housed two orchids and a selection of exquisite
artefacts that Antonio had collected over his years of
travel. Amy swivelled her chair around so that she was
facing him. The neat little navy-blue skirt she was wearing
felt peculiar and she was vaguely aware that it rode up
her thighs just a little too much for her liking.

'I have studied the figures and have reached the obvious
conclusion that your reckless indulging in altruistic projects will have to come to an end.'

'There's nothing reckless about—'

Rocco held up one imperious hand. 'Which is not to
say that I am a monster who does not appreciate the necessity to have a social conscience. However, I think you
will agree that there is a far simpler way of helping.'

'What's that?'

'I am prepared to agree to a set sum that will be given
to charities of your choice.'

Amy looked at him with her mouth half open in stunned
surprise, then she drew in a deep, steadying breath and
said slowly, 'It's so easy for you, isn't it? Need to prove
you have a social conscience? Why, then, just fling a bit

of money at a charity and you can sleep peacefully at nights. After all, where's the point in *actually taking any kind of interest* in the community around you? That's just tiresome, unproductive hard work, isn't it? No precious money to be made there, so why waste time investing human resources in it? It doesn't occur to you that there might be some kind of emotional fulfilment to be had from physically *helping other people!*'

Rocco clicked his tongue with impatience and irritation and pushed himself away from the ledge, moving towards her until he was towering over her. Then he leant over with his hands on either side of her chair, caging her in.

'If you're looking for emotional fulfilment, Miss Hogan, then might I suggest that you are in the wrong job. The figures you have been spending lavishly over the years simply do not add up.' He stood up abruptly but continued to look down at her, his intimidating blue eyes narrowed. 'Now let me see exactly what you are working on at the moment. Obviously I will extend some leeway to projects that are currently in the pipeline.' He strode swiftly back to his desk and Amy reluctantly stood up to follow in his wake, clutching her batch of papers.

She had never met a man quite like him. He was as unfeeling and unmoveable as a rock. It came as no great surprise, when she thought about it. After all, what kind of man could mercilessly cut off all ties with his one surviving parent, whatever the reasons?

She edged round the desk and extracted the complex layout for what she was working on.

'This is one of the more run-down council estates in the city centre,' she explained tersely, shoving up the sleeves of her cotton top and propping herself up on both hands. 'There's a high level of single-parent families living here and consequently a lot of disaffected teenagers with nothing to do. It's been a hard slog but we've managed to obtain planning permission to build a youth centre right here…' She pointed to a highlighted dot on the map with one finger and felt all the enthusiasm and energy flowing into her as she contemplated her newest venture.

The residents were all in favour of this project. The tired, despairing mothers saw it as a way of cutting down on the petty crime continually being committed by bored adolescents, and even the kids she had talked to were keen in their own noncommittal, semi-sneering way.

She pulled out more plans of what they had in mind to build. Dee was a qualified architect and had done detailed drawings of what they could achieve given the restrictions of space. She lost sight of the fact that Rocco was an arch enemy to every word she was saying until she had finally finished talking a long while later, at which point cold reality washed back over her and she straightened up.

'This is nothing like flinging money at a charity and leaving them to get on with it,' she said heatedly.

'No. Flinging money at a charity takes an hour or so while this takes several valuable months of time and effort.'

Rocco pushed back his chair and turned to look at her, clasping his hands behind his head.

'But I have to admit you are very…passionate about what you do…'

'We all are.' Had it been necessary to use that particular description for her? she wondered.

'And when it comes to work, passion, in the right place, can be a very good thing. Where do the rest of those people working with you fit in?'

'Those people?'

Rocco recalled the long-haired men and the cropped-haired women and raised his eyebrows to suggest what he thought of them.

Amy read the message and bristled. 'Freddy's a chartered surveyor, Tim and Andy handle all the dealings with the people who need organising to work on turning our projects into reality, Dee's the architect and Marcy's our administrator.'

'And where do *you* fit in?'

'I oversee everything,' Amy said coldly, sensing implied criticism. 'Make sure deadlines are kept, liaise with various councillors, meet with the residents to make sure that their suggestions are being taken on board.' She edged back, watching as he silently tapped his fingers on the desk.

'And this is the only thing you're working on at the moment? Where are the costings?' Amy stepped forward to rifle through the papers, glanced at her watch and caught her breath.

'In there.' She pointed vaguely at the bundle of papers. 'They're mostly estimates, but I'm quite familiar with all the suppliers we now use and we get pretty good deals from them.'

'Run it by me.'

'I can't.' Amy flushed and looked away, before circling round the desk to fetch her bag from the chair. Where had the time gone? She couldn't have been talking for over two hours? It was now after five-thirty and of all the days to lose track of time, this had to be right up there as one of the worst.

'You have already shown your lack of professionalism in failing to come and see me on the pretext that you were too busy and now it appears that you are happy to cut short what could be a very pivotal meeting for you and your staff because…what?'

'I just have to go. I'm sorry.' Amy slung her bag over her shoulder. 'I didn't realise how long I'd been here.'

'Go where?'

'I'm prepared to discuss whatever you want to discuss as far as work goes, Mr Losi, but I'm certainly not prepared to discuss my personal life with you. That's none of your business.' Those cool blue eyes were unnerving though, and Amy knew how things must look from his point of view. Here she was, ready to defend her position with all the ammunition at her disposal just so long as it didn't clash with her personal life. She sighed and dropped her bag onto the chair.

'I…I have a date, actually, and I can't possibly cancel it because I've already cancelled the last three. Sam's got tickets for us to go to see *A Midsummer Night's Dream* at the theatre and I just don't want to let him down. Again.'

Rocco looked at the flushed, embarrassed face and felt a spurt of intense, unfamiliar interest kick-start inside him.

'Also,' she mumbled uncomfortably into the engulfing silence, which she read as yet more mounting, unspoken criticism, 'my car's in for service and Edward can't take me to the theatre. I'm going to have to get a cab and it's always difficult getting one to come this far out of the town centre in summer. Too many tourists around competing for too few taxi drivers.' She contemplated the convoluted journey, which would not really leave her sufficient time to go back to her house and change, and gloomily tried to imagine Sam's expression as he paced the foyer waiting for her. He wouldn't be overjoyed. He had already told her that her workaholic tendencies were beginning to try his patience.

'Okay.' Rocco shrugged and stood up. 'We'll continue this on Monday.'

Amy breathed a sigh of relief and stole a surreptitious look at him. For a big man, he moved with surprising grace and she wondered whether he played a lot of sport. Didn't they all do that in New York? Join gyms so that they could frantically work out? If he played any sport, she imagined that it would be of the confrontational kind, something like squash that was fast and vigorous and would allow him to thrash his opponent to a pulp.

As far as Amy was concerned, the gym was something that she had spent the past five years meaning to get around to but never quite managing.

She hardly noticed that he was standing beside her, opening the door for her to leave, and she said, in some surprise, 'You're not leaving work already, are you? Don't you burn the midnight oil?'

'What makes you think that I'm not leaving here so that I can carry on burning it somewhere else?' he asked with a crooked smile. The first smile she had seen and her heartbeat quickened treacherously. Bastard the man might be, but a very sexy one.

'In which case, have fun.' She shrugged, heading for the stairs, and was taken aback to find that he was keeping step with her, tailoring his long strides to match her smaller ones.

There were still a number of people in the old building, but most of the secretarial staff had already left. Unofficially, they were allowed to head home earlier than usual on a Friday, and most of the junior members of staff took advantage of the fact. Busy doing the things she had never really seemed to do, she supposed. Partying, flitting from boyfriend to boyfriend, drinking until the early hours of the morning and then waking up with hangovers.

Her father's deteriorating and agonising illness had taken a huge dent out of her youth and she had emerged with all the carefree joys of being young seemingly lost to her for ever. Not that she had once regretted the reasons she had grown into adulthood before her time. She didn't. But she knew that things might have been different if she had not had to cope with the strains of looking after her father when she had barely been able to look after herself. She had thrown herself into her work, knowing that she had had a lot to prove with her age being against her.

'Where are you going?' she asked casually as they walked down the staircase, for the sake of saying something. 'Anywhere interesting?'

'To the theatre,' he said, as casually. 'To drop you off for your hot date.'

Amy stopped dead in her tracks and looked at him with nervous dismay. 'Thank you. Very much, but I'd really rather you didn't.'

'Why not?'

A thousand and one reasons fluttered inside her head but she was hard pressed to name one and, in the ensuing silence, he said reasonably, 'We spent longer than we thought going over the files. That was my fault. Hence I intend to help you make up for lost time by driving you to wherever you are going. Unless you have time to go back to your place and dress first, in which case I'll take the necessary detour, but I should think you probably wouldn't.'

'There's no need to put yourself out…'

'Why don't you accept the offer of a lift in the spirit in which it was intended?'

Amy accepted faintly, faced with zero choice, but the thought of being in a small, enclosed space with this man, *her enemy*, she reminded herself, made her feel unaccountably uneasy.

'I rarely pay attention to the time,' Rocco said, zapping

open the doors of his rented Jaguar with his remote. He opened the passenger door for her and she shot inside like a bolt.

He picked up the easy conversation once he was inside, turning to her with an unreadable expression. 'I usually expect everyone else to abide by the same rules.'

'I don't normally clock-watch, Mr Losi…' Amy's voice trailed off and she was held reluctant captive to his dark, averted profile as he manoeuvred the car out of the court-yard and through the stone columns that fronted the building.

'Hence the three cancelled dates…? And by the way, I think we can do away with the formality of surnames. I always try and encourage a certain amount of informality in my staff. That way, they can feel more relaxed about approaching me.'

Amy tried to equate relaxation with Rocco Losi. The two didn't go together at all. He was just too forbidding. Even now, when he had taken off his intimidating hat, she still couldn't begin to relax in his company. Did he really expect her to? she wondered. After he had told her in no uncertain terms what he intended to do with her precious subsidiary? Trample it into the ground like a cockroach under his foot?

'What changes do you have in mind for the company? Will there be redundancies?'

'What time do you have to be at the theatre?'

'You haven't answered my question.'

'Nor should I.' He glanced swiftly across at her. 'It would be highly unprofessional to discuss something like that with one person. Tell me about your boyfriend. I didn't expect you to have one.'

Amy was distracted enough by the bald rudeness of that to forget all about work, possible redundancies including her own and the collapse of the career she had spent the past decade building up.

'I don't believe you just said that.'

'Why?' Rocco shrugged.

'Because…because *it's rude!*' Rude and insulting and hurtful. 'But why should I be surprised?' she lashed out, still stinging from the bare-faced effrontery. 'You're the most obnoxious, arrogant, rude individual I've ever come across!'

'Funny. That's not an accusation any woman has ever levelled at me in the past…' The air between them throbbed with a violent, hidden charge. He could almost taste her breathless anger raging beneath the prim little outfit that she was obviously uncomfortable wearing.

'Which says a lot about the kind of women you surround yourself with!' The conversation had become disastrously unfocused, but Amy found that it was almost impossible to gather herself together and revert to talking about work. She wanted to wipe that calm, smug, amused expression off his face. 'I'm twenty-six! Believe it or not, most twenty-six-year-old women do not live in a physical vacuum!' For a second, she wondered who she was trying to convince, him or herself. She had had boyfriends, well, three of them, but none had ever come close to distracting her from her work. She had certainly never been the sort of girl who had led a wild, abandoned sexual life, but to be casually dismissed by this man as a nonentity who had surprised him by having a boyfriend was hateful and wounding.

'No,' he agreed, in an aggravatingly reasonable voice. 'I just assumed that you were one of these women who puts her career first.'

'I don't just think about work!' But she did, she acknowledged silently. She had been forced to become too self-sufficient from too young an age, and she had transferred all the needs that most normal people expended on relationships into her work. In some weird way, she was as emotionally detached as Rocco Losi.

'So what's he like, this man?'

'Do you know how to get to the theatre? You're so busy nosing into my private life that you might just end up missing the turnings.'

'I'm not nosing into your private life, Amy. I'm conversing with you on a subject that has nothing to do with work.'

The way he said her name sent a little shiver racing down her spine, but when she looked at him it was with resentment and apprehension.

'You want to take my job away from me. You want to make me and my team unemployed. How can you calmly sit there and pretend to be interested in having a normal conversation?'

'I want to do what benefits the company in the long run,' Rocco said tersely.

'Why?'

'Why what?'

Still smarting from the unpleasant way he had of thoroughly unsettling her, Amy forgot about the little fact that he was her boss and she was simply an inconvenient employee on her way out. Her normal reasonable, pragmatic character that made her so good at what she did seemed to have given way to a driving need to say something or do something that would get under his skin the way he managed to get under hers.

'Why do you care one way or another what happens to Losi Construction?' she blurted out. 'It's not as though you've ever taken the slightest bit of interest in it!'

The silence stretched like taut wire and Amy wrestled

with the desire to apologise for overstepping the boundaries and a feeling that she could say just as she damn well pleased. He, obviously, felt that he could make whatever remarks he wanted to about things that didn't concern him and, anyway, it was hardly as though she had very much to lose.

She still felt horribly nervous in the wake of her outburst, though, and even more nervous when he pulled the car over to the side and killed the engine.

'What are you doing?' she asked, biting her lower lip and watching him warily, the way one might watch a tiger that had been recently fed but might still fancy a bit more.

'Developing this conversation,' Rocco told her, angling his big body so that he was facing her.

Supplies of oxygen suddenly seemed to plummet. 'Sorry if I spoke out of place,' Amy said grudgingly, 'but you *did* say that you liked your employees to be on a first-name basis with you so that they could feel free to air any grievances...'

'And your grievance is...?'

'That you've got your own life in New York. That you've never troubled yourself with your father or with his company and yet you think that you can just storm in now, take control, change people's lives for ever and then sweep back out leaving everyone to pick up the pieces and carry on!'

'You're over-dramatising.'

'Am I?' Amy snorted in disbelief and was more rattled by his lack of fight than if he had picked up the heated gauntlet she had thrown down and engaged in his usual warfare.

'I have no intention of chucking every member of staff out on their ears,' he objected mildly. 'Just tidying things up a bit and the reason why is because that's just the way

I'm built. We do have a bit in common, come to think of it. We both had to climb the ladder step by painful step, without help from anyone.'

'I *had* to,' Amy said, tilting her chin. 'You *chose* to. And besides, you had the help of a university education! I had GCSE qualifications and desperation!'

Desperate was exactly how she was feeling now, skewered to the car door by those hooded blue eyes. Every breath she took was laborious.

'You've invested everything into your job, haven't you?' he asked softly and Amy stubbornly refused to answer. She was trying hard to bring herself back down to earth and establish the dislike and animosity that had fuelled her emotions towards the silver-tongued devil staring at her with those amazing eyes, but it was a bit like trying to remain upright on a bed of quicksand.

'That's why, at twenty-six, you're not in any solid relationship—'

'I told you—'

'That you have a boyfriend. One you're seeing tonight out of guilt because you've broken the last three engagements on the pretext of work.'

'I'm not seeing Sam out of guilt!' Her cheeks reddened as she uncomfortably wondered whether his random stab had hit closer to the target than she would have expected. 'And anyway, are you going to drop me at the theatre? Because if not, then please tell me and I'll just get out and walk the rest of the way.'

'You'll walk for three miles in uncomfortable shoes out of pride?'

'Got it in one.'

She looked away and heard him laugh, a rich, full sound that made the nerves in her body come alive, but then he started the engine and pulled away while she dealt with her hammering heart with a stern dose of frozen silence.

'I think you might just do it as well...' Rocco murmured lazily. 'Men don't like that, you know...'

'Don't like what? Women who are prepared to walk now and again if it's necessary? Or women who actually have one or two principles that they're prepared to stand up for?'

'Oh, hard-nosed women who like to be in control. Women who are so busy shouting and venting their spleen about what they believe in that they never take time out to listen to what other people have to say...'

'Thanks. Thank you very much for that piece of advice. Coming from a man who doesn't seem to have time to listen to what other people have to say, I'll make sure that I take what you say on board.'

'Of course,' Rocco drawled, noticing with a twinge of regret that they were approaching the theatre, 'those types of women tend to attract the same kind of man...'

'Any point in me telling you that I'm not really the slightest bit interested in what you have to say on the subject?'

'Weak men. Men who enjoy being bullied about and bossed around. Men who don't mind being stood up continually.'

Amy waited until he had pulled over to the pavement and then turned to him. 'I'll roughly translate that into men who listen to what people try to say to them. Unlike you. You've written off what I do and my contribution to the company without even bothering to go into too many details. You took one look at the balance sheet and then decided that we just weren't profitable and so had to be eliminated. If that's the mark of a strong man, then, frankly, I think I prefer the weak ones.' Amy was quite proud of this heartfelt speech. Her voice had been calm and composed and he would have to have been a mind-reading genius to guess at how angry she was at his un-invited generalisations made at her expense. If this was his idea of polite, non-work-oriented conversation, then she was surprised that he had a social life at all.

'What details did you have in mind? There's just so much one can do with a list of figures, most of them in the outgoing column.'

'Well, you could come and see for yourself what we do!' Amy opened the car door, stepped out of the car, then said, leaning into it, 'Or are you one of these strong men who refuse to budge once they've made their minds up?'

Rocco had to hand it to her—she wasn't going to take her medicine lying down. Naturally, she wouldn't win. There were too many hard facts stacked up against her, whether she liked to believe it or not, but he was nothing if not fair. He would go and have a look at her little pet project and then no one would be able to accuse him of being bull-headed when he was regrettably forced to shut the enterprise down.

CHAPTER THREE

THE play was good. Dinner, afterwards with Sam, some-what less so. Amy made the mistake of confiding in him about the newest addition to the company and what it meant in terms of her work being summarily terminated, and was regaled with his self-righteous outrage for most of the pizza meal.

The altruistic fervour that had drawn her to him three months previously left her feeling flat and confused.

'I don't think he's too bothered by the concept of help-ing the community,' Amy explained, pushing away her plate. Now stone-cold, her pizza resembled something that had been fashioned out of Play-Doh.

'Typical mogul,' Sam snorted. 'Met a lot of those my-self. Only interested in making money. Would drop a bomb over a council estate if they thought they could rebuild it into five-bedroom executive homes that they could sell at inflated prices to a gullible public.'

'Well, maybe not quite as dramatic as that...' Amy smiled and tried to defuse some of the unpleasant feeling.

She had met Sam quite accidentally while working on her previous project. He worked in an organisation spe-cialising in care in the community and they had clicked immediately, finding that they had quite a bit in common when it came to their natural empathy towards good causes. Almost without realising it, their friendship had developed into something more, though what, precisely, she wasn't altogether sure. But she was happy enough to go along for the ride. He might not be the most striking person she had ever encountered in the looks department, with his thinning sandy hair and pale blue eyes, but he was comfortable and thoughtful and genuinely interested in all the things she was genuinely interested in.

She looked at his kind, earnest face and a darker, far more dangerous one superimposed itself on her retina.

Sam was now expounding on the many different businessmen he had met over the years and the superhuman efforts it took to get them interested in the community that was as important to them as they were to it. Money, he was fervently saying, while making sure to finish his pizza that looked every bit as off-putting as her own half-finished one, was the root of all evil.

'I'm too tired to think about this,' Amy said, stifling a yawn. 'Anyway, he's agreed to come along with me to have a look at what we're working on at the moment. Maybe I can change his mind.'

'And if you can't?'

'Then I shall be out of a job, along with my staff.'

'What would you do?'

'Find another.'

'They're pretty thin on the ground, Amy, jobs like that. In fact, yours is unique. You can do what you enjoy doing and you're funded for it. What could be better?' He ordered two coffees without asking her whether she wanted one and sat back as they were brought to the table.

The weight of her pressurised day was getting to her. She could easily have rested her head in her hands and nodded off to sleep.

Sam was busily expounding on the huge benefits of doing what she did while Amy half listened and found herself thinking of how Rocco would react when he found himself traipsing around sites with her. Would he be bored? Indifferent? Would he feign interest? He was an immensely successful businessman. He would have feigning interest down to an art form. Then she thought that he certainly hadn't feigned any interest in her plight. No need to. So she was back to imagining him with a bored, irritable expression and only half caught the tail-end of Sam's remark.

'I mean,' he obligingly repeated for her benefit, 'there would be no need then for you to get something as demanding as what you're doing now. You could work part-time, perhaps. Maybe even in the capacity of a volunteer...'

'Sam. I don't know what you're talking about. Sorry. I'm just so tired. My thoughts were a million miles away.'

He looked annoyed and it flashed through her mind that that was one of his less endearing traits. He never actually blew his top but he could be sulky and petulant when things didn't go his way, as he would have been if she had cancelled on him again.

'I *was saying*,' he stressed, 'that we could take things a step further.'

'A step further?' The coffee that had been ordered on her behalf, which she hadn't wanted, now seemed a brilliant focus for her distraction.

'I think we should get engaged.'

'You think *we should get engaged?* After three months?'

'Knowing someone for years doesn't necessarily mean a good marriage,' Sam said testily. 'I'm thirty-eight. I want to settle down, Amy, and I think I've found the right girl to settle down with. Someone who shares my interests, enjoys the simple pleasures in life.' He reached over and enfolded her hand in his. 'We do get along, don't we?'

'Yes, we do,' Amy agreed, struggling to give his suggestion houseroom and feeling hunted in the process. 'But I don't want to rush into anything.' She squeezed his hand and then tactfully withdrew hers.

'Promise me you'll think about it.'

'Of course.' She tried to picture being Sam's wife. He would be a good husband, steady, reliable and would, one day, be a very good father. And they had a lot in common. 'But I'm only twenty-six…'

'Time waits for no man.' He fell back on a cliché, and then was happy to change the conversation, to chat about the play and compare it to the other Shakespeare production they had seen two months previously.

Amy didn't think, however, that his proposal would go away, that she could put it to the back of a cupboard and carry on with their undemanding, soothing relationship, even when two days later she told him that she really couldn't commit to an answer, not just yet, not when there was so much stress in her life at the moment.

Rocco, unsurprisingly, hadn't beaten a path to her door to be shown around her project in progress. She wondered whether he figured she and her project would just conveniently vanish into thin air. Or, more likely, his silence was a pointed way of informing her that, whatever she did, she would not be able to face him down, so what was the point in him bothering to look around anything with her?

Antonio was slowly recovering, to the extent that he could now engage in conversation for a few minutes at a time, but she was under no illusions that she could tell him what was happening to his company. The consultant had emphasised the need to protect him from undue stress.

So the previous day, when she had snatched an hour over lunch to visit him, she had been forced to wear a bright smile and pretend that everything was all right, and in a sense it had been worth it to see the relief on his face. It was only when she was going that she'd asked, casually, whether he was happy that his son was back home now, that bridges had been mended, even if the circumstances had been wrong.

'Mended?' Antonio had laughed shortly. 'Nothing has been mended. The boy is back under duress. To tell you the truth, I have not seen him for more than five minutes at a time. He comes as a formality to make sure that I have not died overnight.'

That was enough to fire her up into phoning Rocco first thing the following morning.

'I hope you haven't forgotten that you promised to look around my site with me,' she opened, deciding straight away that if he could ignore the simple rules of conversational courtesy, then so could she.

Rocco leaned back in his chair, phone pressed to his ear, and smiled into the receiver. He hadn't forgotten. He had just decided that a few days of silence would give her breathing space to contemplate the inevitable. He had also known that sooner or later she would call. She was nothing if not tenacious. But having her call would immediately and subconsciously put her in an inferior position. She was dealing with a master of the game. Rocco had more psychological tricks up his sleeve than a state-of-the-art conjurer had rabbits up his hat, and he used them with ruthless certainty.

He also appreciated her blunt opening. Her way, he supposed, of putting him in his place. The secretary tapped on his door and poked her head into the room and he immediately waved her away, then he swivelled his chair around so that it was facing the window and he could see the sprawling view outside.

'Did you enjoy your play?' he asked.

'Yes, it was very good, thank you. Were you being serious about coming with me to see my project firsthand or were you just humouring me?'

'Oh, yes. I'll see if I can set something up in my diary, shall I?'

'There's a meeting with some of the residents at eight o'clock tomorrow night. That would be the best time. You could meet the people face to face, the people whose lives are going to be changed by what we're doing. You could talk to some of them, perhaps, and get a feel for what we're really all about.'

Before she could get going into one of those holier-than-thou moments, Rocco interrupted, 'Fine.' There was a local directors' dinner planned for seven-thirty at one of the hotels, which promised to be deadly. He would scrap that and send Martins in his place. There was company involvement and then there was going beyond the bounds of duty, and chatting over some half-baked meal somewhere with people he would not be dealing with in the long-term future fell solidly into that category.

And besides…

Rocco stuck his long legs onto the window ledge and thought of one very earnest, lightly freckled face with fiery eyes and a tongue to match…

'I'll pick you up at your house at what…seven? Seven-thirty?'

'There's no need.'

'Has your car come out of service yet? Or do you intend to let your pride push you into taking public transport?'

'Make it seven-fifteen.' She gave him her address and then basic directions of how to get to her house, which was midway between his office and the city centre. 'You *will* turn up, won't you?' she asked bluntly.

'Oh, I'll be there. Although…just out of curiosity, what would you *do* if I failed to show up?'

'Be disappointed but not entirely shocked and I would make my own way there.'

Touché, Rocco thought, with a lazy smile.

He made arrangements for his replacement immediately and found that he was actually looking forward to trailing around the project, which would be her last.

'You're living in cloud-cuckoo-land if you think you stand a chance of changing the man's mind,' was the first thing Sam said when she telephoned him the following afternoon to tell him how she would be spending her evening.

Amy stifled a sigh of irritation and took herself off to the bathroom, phone in hand, so that she could start running a bath.

'I prefer to be optimistic.'

'Then brace yourself for a huge disappointment, Amy. I told you, I've met men like that before when I've been out there fund-raising.'

Amy idly thought that it was very doubtful whether he had ever met anyone like Rocco Losi in his life before, but she refrained from making the remark. She was just grateful that he had not broached the subject of what they had spoken about a few days before, respecting her desire to mull over his proposal. Which she had, in no way, mulled over.

She let him lecture to her, having lost the energy to argue back, and was thoughtful when she finally replaced the receiver fifteen minutes later and stepped into the bath.

An uneasy voice inside her head was telling her that Sam, perhaps, would not really mind that much if she lost her job, if Rocco did what he wanted to do and axed her department. Out of a job, she would be vulnerable.

Then she laughed at herself for thinking like that when she, of all people, knew just how kind-hearted a man Sam was.

Unlike Rocco Losi, who probably wouldn't know an act of kindness if it lunged at him and grabbed him by the throat.

Half an hour till he was due to show up and, while most of her expected him to, there was still a little part gearing itself for his non-appearance. Which hardly explained why she was being a bit more careful with her appearance than she usually was.

Jeans, of course, because she would be an utter idiot to show up for a residents' meeting on a rough council estate in a suit, but instead of her usual trainers she slung on a pair of tan loafers that were just as comfortable but somehow managed to upgrade the outfit. And she bypassed the functional baggy, cotton sweatshirt in favour of a ribbed, tight-fitting one that matched the loafers. Then she brushed her hair until it shone and dabbed on just the merest hint of lipstick.

She was ready and waiting when the doorbell rang at precisely seven-fifteen, making her think that he must be a whizz at timing his journeys.

'Surprised to see me?' was the first thing he asked when she swung the door open and stepped outside. It was still light, but not as warm as it had been during the day, and he was dressed casually for the weather, in some khaki trousers and a black cotton jumper. Out of his working clothes, he was even more impressive than in them, and Amy caught herself unable to speak just for a few seconds, then her thought processes swung back into gear and she quietly pulled the door shut behind her and locked it.

'Not at all. I knew you would want to see the work we

do before reaching a decision about disposing of it.' They walked towards his car and she suddenly stopped.

'You came in *this?*' His Jaguar was like a shiny beacon among the pedestrian cars lining the kerb.

'What else did you expect me to come in?' Rocco asked politely. 'A rickshaw?'

'I didn't think. You can't possible drive us there in this.'

'Why not?' His voice was impatient but Amy remained where she was with her arms folded. 'In case it had slipped your mind, I delivered you to the theatre in this. As far as I know, it runs perfectly smoothly. Shouldn't be a problem getting us to wherever it is we're going.' She was staring at it as though it were coated in a highly infectious agent and his irritability went up a couple more notches. Weren't women supposed to be impressed with sleek, fast motors? 'Just get in, would you?'

'We're going to a deprived council estate,' Amy explained, looking at him steadily. 'Point one, I don't think it's appropriate for us to arrive in this kind of car, and point two, it'll end up being targeted.'

'Point three…' Rocco looked around him as if looking for something and then repositioned his eyes firmly on her face '…there's no handy replacement car waiting for us in the wings as far as I can see, so we're just going to have to chance it. Alternatively, I could leave you here, you could make your own way to this residents' meeting and you could forget all thoughts of me coming along with you at another time to see this project of yours.'

Which neatly tied her up.

'Okay.' Amy shrugged and slung open the car door. 'But don't blame me if something happens to it.'

'I won't,' Rocco assured her, getting in and firing the

engine. 'Now, give me the directions and let's get this over and done with.'

'I'm not force-feeding you nasty medicine, Mr Losi…'

'Stop calling me by my surname.'

'Oh, sorry. Forgot. You favour the informal approach. Just follow this road straight till I tell you where to turn.'

'If this council estate is so rough, how do you make out?' Rocco asked curiously. The women he met were not ambitious when it came to exploring territories they were unfamiliar with. The career women moved with ease in the skyscraper jungle of New York but probably would have no idea what the other side of the tracks looked like, and the women he dated…well, he doubted any of them had ever travelled on the underground, never mind actually gone into a district that did not sport designer clothes shops and trendy restaurants. He slid a sidelong glance at the woman sitting upright next to him and was shocked to find his eyes straying downwards from her face to her breasts, which were nicely outlined against the top she was wearing.

'I feel comfortable there. Well, most of the time. I wouldn't be doing what I did if I was scared of venturing on a council estate.'

'And your boyfriend doesn't worry?'

'Of course he doesn't worry!' Amy looked across at him, startled. 'Why should he?'

'I would have thought that might have been obvious. His woman doing a job that took her to places where a car like this might be trashed…'

His woman. The phrase was old-fashioned, chauvinistic and staggeringly possessive. All those traits, in fact, which she positively loathed, but when spoken by him sent a little feminine shiver racing up her spine.

'I'm perfectly capable of looking after myself. I'm not of the clinging-vine variety.'

A raging feminist, he translated in his head. Just the sort of woman he would normally do his utmost to avoid except in a boardroom where they could be as tough as any man. In a life that was intensely pressured, he preferred to relax in the company of women who didn't demand too high a standard of conversation.

Amy was looking at him narrowly. 'Sam knows that he doesn't have to cluck around me like a mother hen every time I go out on a job.'

'Even when those jobs take you to potentially dangerous areas…'

'We're not talking about heading off for the front line in a war zone,' she said with heavy sarcasm and he grinned. Did he know how much younger he looked when he smiled? With those obvious looks, he probably had a high hit-rate with women and she wondered what he was like when he went into action, when he turned on the charm that was firmly reined in whenever he happened to find himself in her company. 'Anyway, it's just a matter of being sensible. I wouldn't go to a meeting in the depths of winter, at night, to some of the places I would visit during the day with Freddy or Tim.'

'Freddy being the ponytailed New Age chap who works with you?'

'Freddy being the qualified chartered surveyor who came in the top twenty in the country when he took his final exams, yes. When you get to the next roundabout, you'll have to take the first turning left, follow the road to the top and then keep straight on. The estate is just on the left. You can't miss it.'

Understatement of the decade, Rocco thought. It loomed grimly threatening against a backdrop of sparse shrubbery here and there and the odd despairing tree. The sun was beginning to fade but there was no avoiding the fact that here was a collection of cell-block-like edifices, some randomly sporting graffiti, in which not much would be encouraged to thrive.

Rocco lived in an apartment, which was in a block that rose far higher than any of these concrete buildings, but there all comparison ended. He enjoyed the magnificent luxuries that only vast sums of money could buy. The twenty-four-hour porter service, the fabulous reception area on the ground floor, his own private lift, a sports complex that spanned one entire floor in which every member of staff was devoted to the comfort of their extremely wealthy tenants.

'Where do you suggest I park?'

Amy tried not to smirk and failed. 'The entrance is behind the estate. I *did* warn you about the car.'

'Not that you would ever dream of saying *I told you so*.' Rocco gave in to her victory with good grace.

He was as far out of his rarefied world as it was possible to get and he could only watch, impressed, over the next hour as she comfortably took the lead, joking easily with the gang of twelve strong teenagers who congregated around the car as soon as it was parked. She asked them what they had been up to, addressed most by name, introduced him in passing, making sure to quickly move on with the good-natured conversation before they could home in on the stranger in their midst.

He still didn't trust them around his car, but grudgingly had to admit that they seemed more impressed than intent on inflicting damage.

Freddy and two of the other members of staff were already there and the meeting was rowdy, with strong contributions from nearly every resident who had shown up, which was in the region of eighty. Amy chaired, Marcy took notes, barely looking up to see what was going on, and as things began to wind down he heard Amy introduce him loudly to everyone.

He stood up, commanding instant attention from a silent crowd, and shot her a 'nice one' look to which she responded with a 'don't know what you mean' flash in her eyes.

Years of experience in public speaking made him swing into action without hesitation as he took the floor. He had addressed packed halls full of the great and the good, had held meetings in which the top men in the world of business had listened attentively. Never had he addressed a crowd of mainly females, many with kids in tow, who were waiting to bombard him with every question under the sun.

And Amy had to hand it to him. He rose to the occasion. There was the odd light remark, but he spoke fluently on the need to build and look forward, to gather resources however grim the surroundings and see light at the end of a tunnel. No round of applause. That wasn't the style of these people, but their silence was telling. Anyone less impressive would have been jeered off without a moment's hesitation.

'Thank you very much for that,' he said as soon as everyone had dispersed and they were on their own again. In the space of time they had been inside, darkness had descended. The teenagers had gone and the car appeared to be in one piece, no missing wheels or hubcaps.

'You did very well,' Amy said truthfully.

'And your feeling is…? Intense disappointment?'

'Sorry, but I couldn't resist. Do you know how to get out of here or shall I direct you?'

'Nothing quite like enlisting one hundred per cent involvement from the unconvinced, is there?'

Amy laughed, relaxed and still on that peculiar high that she always got when she had been immersed in her work. 'And are you convinced now? Did you mean all that stuff about aspiring to rise above surroundings and trying to build something when everything else is falling down around you? Or was it all a load of tosh because you'd been caught like a worm on a hook?'

'What you're planning to do isn't going to turn that estate into a crime-free zone, full of enthusiastic, well-behaved teenagers who suddenly want to become doctors and teachers.'

'God, why are you so cynical?'

'I don't call it cynical. I call it realistic. I'm taking you out for a meal. What kind of food do you enjoy eating?'

The thought of going out for something to eat with him brought an immediate feeling of excitement. It shot through her like poison. 'Thanks, but I'd rather you just dropped me back home, actually. It's late and I'm tired.' She belatedly thought of Sam, dear Sam who would have a fit if he thought that she was dining out with her enemy.

'Have you eaten?'

'I had something a bit earlier on,' Amy said shortly.

'A bit earlier on...*when?*'

'A bit earlier on at lunchtime, OK?'

'Nothing since then?'

'Look, Rocco—' she twisted round so that she was facing him, ready for an argument to cover up the intense excitement she had felt at his average, reasonable offer to take her for something to eat and her guilt when she imagined Sam's face should he ever find out '—I'm not hungry. We've done what we set out to do. You saw what we're working on, you spoke to the residents, now it's time to go home. Tomorrow I'll put everything in a report and I hope you'll be bothered to read it.' Here was a man who wanted to take away everything she cared about, everything she had spent years working so hard to build up. How could she be attracted to him? How? She hated herself for her weakness, she who had always staunchly maintained that the power of physical attraction was worthless.

'No deal,' Rocco said calmly, following signs to the city centre.

'*No deal?* How *dare* you?'

'Firstly because this is my car, which I am driving, and secondly because *you* may not be hungry since you nibbled something several hours ago, but *I* most certainly am. So dinner we shall have and if you don't state a preference…' ah, signs to a car park '…then you'll just have to fall in with me. Right now I favour Italian.' He swung into the multi-storey car park, blithely ignoring her simmering resentment at his total takeover.

'Take me home *at once!*'

'Stop behaving like a child.'

Amy spluttered, lost for words at the sheer nerve of what he had just said.

'I'm taking you out for dinner because neither of us has had anything to eat for hours and it's now nine-thirty. I'm not launching a physical assault on you.'

Which sent another treacherous tingle leaping through her. 'I don't think Sam would like it if he knew that we were having dinner together,' she said. He wouldn't be jealous. That wasn't Sam's thing at all. He wasn't the jealous type, which was good, she told herself, because it showed trust. No, he wouldn't like it because he would feel that she should keep Rocco at an arm's length. There was *them* and there was *us*, he had told her more than once. *Them* were all those people who couldn't understand the importance of what they did, who thought that big business and making money were the only things worth sweating for. Rocco was definitely one of *them*. For Sam, the business of trying to persuade him would be acceptable. The business of fraternising with him would be a betrayal.

'Oh?' Rocco slotted the car neatly into a vacant space, switched off the engine and turned to her, eyebrows raised in dry enquiry. 'But I thought that he was one of those liberal, non-possessive types who didn't cluck around you like a mother hen?'

Amy glared at him, turned away and slammed the car door behind her as she got out.

'Well?' Rocco persisted in a voice that was laced with amusement.

'I think Sam would rather I were having dinner with *him*,' Amy said, head held high.

'That could be easily arranged. Why don't you call him and invite him along for the ride? Better still, I could call him just in case he got the mistaken impression that I might not welcome his company. In fact…' Rocco flicked his cell phone out of his pocket '…I would love to meet your boyfriend. I have always found that it's a good idea to get to know more than just the superficial details of my employees. Makes them three-dimensional, real people instead of just faceless worker bees…'

Rocco found that he wasn't actually lying. He was surprisingly curious about this mystery man about whom the woman striding along next to him was so unforthcoming. Women were normally so terminally drawn to rambling on about their men, to showing them off along with the diamonds sitting on their fingers, to wandering around with a dreamy look in their eyes and a faraway expression of bliss.

Rocco took a keen interest in all his employees. His ability for recall was limitless, as was his wry observation of those female members of his staff who fell in love and turned swiftly from eight-to-whenevers into nine-to-fivers who couldn't wait to race home to their men.

'Italian would be fine.' Amy tried to imagine how Sam and Rocco would interact and came to the conclusion that Rocco would eat Sam alive. As spectator sports went, that was one she had no intention of indulging in.

Which left her in no position to continue harping on about wanting to go home.

They had emerged from the car park into a pleasantly cool evening with the smells and sounds of summer around them. There were lots of people around, couples, groups, all laughing and relaxed in the late evening. This was obviously the hub of restaurants and night life.

For the moment, Rocco was content to drop the little matter of her boyfriend, knowing that, the more he probed, the faster she would retreat, especially since she knew that his probing was founded in nothing more meaningful than idle curiosity. Instead, he asked her about the place and Amy snatched the change of topic to tell him everything she knew about what had been happening in the city centre, finishing with, 'Didn't you ever have any interest in visiting the place? In the past ten years?'

'No.' One syllable spoken with such flat finality that she glanced across to him in surprise.

'Oh, sorry. Sensitive subject, I take it.'

'Yes,' he grated, steering her into the first Italian they came across, only to discover that there were no tables free for at least half an hour. 'We'll wait,' he said shortly. 'And in case you hadn't got the message,' Rocco said, finally facing her squarely, eyes narrowed, 'my private life is off limits.'

Amy waited until he had ordered a glass of wine for them both. 'And my private life isn't?'

Rocco gave her a thunderous frown from his ten-inch height advantage. 'I can't remember asking you anything very personal,' he said with an edgy threat in his voice, even though the cooler part of him was telling him to leave it alone and move on to a less contentious topic of conversation. 'I also find nosy, prying women highly ir-ritating.'

'Oh, dear,' Amy said, enjoying the feeling of somehow catching him on the back foot. 'Nosy. Prying. Would that mean asking the odd question or two?' She gazed serenely up at him and his intense blue eyes sent a bolt of sheer giddy thrill rocketing through her. She quickly gulped a couple of mouthfuls of wine.

'That's right. The odd question or two on the wrong subject.' Rocco never, but never, discussed his past with anyone. The few women who had tried to worm their way into his affections by expressing interest in his back-ground had met with a brick wall and had instantly re-treated.

He looked, ill temperedly, at the face staring up at him and met her direct gaze without flinching.

She might not meet the normal standards of the highly feminine women he was accustomed to. The flirtatious ways of the female sex might have bypassed her, but he was still her boss and he would make damn sure to say as much if her tongue decided to wander in the wrong direction…

CHAPTER FOUR

AMY finished her glass of wine, which must really have been a tiny glass considering she polished it off in under five minutes when she wasn't a drinker. She rested it on the bar and nodded without hesitation to the offer of another.

Like her, Sam was not a big drinker. He didn't exactly view alcohol as the product of the devil, but his mother had always expressed distaste for people who never knew when to stop, and her words had somehow entered his system through a process of osmosis. Since Amy had never taken much interest in alcohol, it had been just something else that they seemed to have in common.

This wine, she thought guiltily, must be particularly good or else especially weak if she wanted another already.

Maybe it was just addictively strong, she thought, nursing the glass as they were led to their table and she found that her legs were feeling a lot less steady than they were accustomed to.

'So, let me get this straight,' she said as soon as she was thankfully seated and no longer had to worry about the state of her legs or anything else. 'You don't like women to be too assertive, you prefer them to look up to you as a caveman style he-man who sees them as his property and, in addition, you'd rather they never asked too many questions that were too personal...'

Rocco was hit by the feeling that this was one of the few moments in his life when he was utterly lost for words. Amy, already halfway through her second glass of wine and feeling better for it by the second, jumped into the brief silence to continue, 'With all those parameters, it must be a little delicate actually making relationships *happen*, I would have thought…'

'Not everyone is quite as…*forceful* as you,' Rocco said heavily.

'I don't think it's particularly forceful to wonder how it is that you never felt inclined to come back and have a look around at the place where you grew up…'

'I did not *grow up* in the centre of Birmingham,' Rocco informed her. 'Actually, I never *lived* in the city centre, so I have no sentimental yearnings to return to it! In fact, at the risk of being pedantic, I have about as much sentimental feeling towards it as I would have towards a random town I had located by sticking a pin on a map.'

Amy sipped her drink and then proceeded to sit on her hands, a childish habit she had never quite lost but that she consciously strove to avoid, 'You mean you *never* ventured into the city, even though you only lived a few miles away?'

'This is a conversation without a future.'

'I was just trying to turn you into a three-dimensional person,' Amy said helpfully, quoting him back neatly, and Rocco exhaled one long sigh of pure exasperation.

'I never actually spent a great deal of time in this part of the country,' he snapped. The ice in his drink had melted and he pushed it aside, virtually untouched.

'Oh, yes. You went to a boarding-school.' For a minute her eyes softened on him, which as far as he was concerned was even worse.

'Information from my father, I presume? During one of your cosy chats? Possibly after you had buttered him up into supporting some hare-brained project that would involve spending buckets of money somewhere for no return?'

Normally Amy would predictably have reacted to this with anger, but the wine had softened her instincts to defend, and, instead of snapping back, she drifted off for a few seconds into pleasant memories of the many evenings she had spent with Antonio, chatting to him about everything under the sun. She leaned forward on her hands and smiled.

'We did spend lots of time chatting,' she admitted, gazing past Rocco's startling face, into her memories. 'I missed that when my father got...ill. Dad and I used to chat a lot. I guess because I was his only child. He treated me much more like an adult than a kid...' She refocused on Rocco's shuttered expression and frowned. How had she arrived at that particular confidence?

'Did you miss home a lot when you were at boarding-school?'

The directness of the question, her obvious disregard for what he had told her about the boundaries he laid down around himself, took him aback and he signalled to the waitress for her to take their order. He would normally thrash anything into the ground, but this time he would have to take the distasteful decision to retreat. It went against every grain in him but he had no choice. His private life was not up for chit-chat over an Italian. Not up for chit-chat period.

'Have you been here before?' he asked politely as he scrutinised the menu.

'Never.'

'Surprising. It's got a very buoyant atmosphere. And the food seems to be good value for money.'

'Oh, we don't often venture into the city for a meal,' Amy explained. 'Easier to stay local.' Maybe she would reconsider that option though. The menu was certainly a lot more appealing than the usual Chinese, Indian or pizza fare she and Sam were used to eating.

'I've been to the city quite a bit, though, and not just through my work. When your dad was fit and healthy, we would sometimes drive in on a weekend. He used to love going to the old Bull Ring.'

'The *market?*' Rocco couldn't contain his surprise at this snippet of information.

'Why do you sound so shocked?'

'I don't recall him ever expressing any interest in going to markets, not unless you consider the food hall at Harvey Nichols a market.' His voice was laced with scorn. 'In fact, from what I remember, he had other people to do the awkward business of shopping for him. I can't imagine him traipsing through a flea-infested pit just for the fun of it.'

'It wasn't a flea-infested pit,' Amy informed him quietly. 'In fact, it was always very lively, full of people selling everything from used books to bales of cloth.' Her face softened. 'He developed a passion for the book stalls, as a matter of fact. So much so that in summer, on a Sunday morning, we would hunt out different open-air markets in the countryside, just so that he could browse through the second-hand book stalls.'

'Looking for what? Something suitably worthwhile which he could buy for a penny and sell for a pound?'

His acidity snapped her out of her mellow, wine-induced mood and she looked at him with unconcealed curiosity. 'You make him sound like a monster.'

'And you make him sound like a saint.'

'Not a saint. But someone very kind, very thoughtful, not too proud to mingle with people socially his inferior or to go to places like markets when he could easily have afforded anything he wanted brand-new and straight out of an expensive shop somewhere.'

That brought a guffaw of harsh laughter. 'Are you sure we are talking about the same man?'

'One you obviously never saw,' Amy told him, braving all the ground rules he had laid down about not treading on his personal territory, 'but maybe one you could have if you'd ever taken the time to make an effort.'

Rocco's face froze. A dark flush spread over his high, sculpted cheekbones and his mouth flattened into a thin, forbidding line.

'How typical of the person with a social conscience,' he said coldly. 'Always there with the woolly, meaningless words of wisdom which they somehow feel they have a God-given duty to express. Ever ready to right the world and preach heartfelt sermons about things they know nothing about.'

'Having a social conscience isn't a crime and, believe me, the last thing I ever do is preach.' She sat back so that their starters could be placed in front of them. A platter of antipasti that was designed to be shared. Cold meats, cold roasted vegetables in olive oil and herbs, tomatoes laced with garlic.

'Really?' Rocco jabbed some of the meat onto his fork and looked at her with distaste. 'Hence your trite little remark about my lack of effort being the source of my misfortunes in not knowing this wonderful old duffer you seem to have unearthed?'

'How can you talk about your father like that?'

'Quite easily considering the man I knew was frozen in ice. A tyrant who expected his only son to address him as *sir* and was prone to towering rages if so much as a scrape of noise was heard in the hallowed walls of the grand old manor from which he presided like a lord over his army of servants.' He stabbed some more meat with his fork, furious with himself for his weakness in explaining anything of his past to the girl looking at him with an unreadable expression. 'So on the point of my father, I think we will have to differ,' he informed her coolly. 'You're not eating.'

Amy obligingly helped herself to some of the vegetables, which tasted of garlic and were mouth-wateringly delicious. What he had just said had left her shaken, but she knew better than to pursue the subject. Instead, she asked him about New York, making sure not to steer into any more dangerously private waters, although her curiosity was overwhelming.

'Why did you choose New York, of all places, to live?' she finally asked. 'Why not Italy? Wouldn't it have been easier to have just returned to your country of birth if you wanted to start from the bottom?'

'Italy was not an option,' Rocco said bluntly.

'Oh.' Pause. 'Why not?'

'Do you ever stop asking questions?' he grated and she smiled with such disarming frankness that he was nearly tempted to smile back.

'It's a habit,' Amy explained truthfully. 'I ask questions all the time. It's part and parcel of what I do. How else do I find out what people need if I don't ask questions?'

'And what do *you* need?'

'You already know.'

'Do I?' For a few disorienting seconds as the almond-brown eyes met his Rocco had the mistaken impression that they were talking about something else entirely. Whenever the word *need* was spoken by a woman in his presence, it only ever had one answer. *Him.*

'My job,' she said prosaically. 'To continue doing what I do. I know you think it's ridiculous for your father to

have subsidised building projects for the needy, that help-
ing other people is a waste of good resources, but it's
very worthwhile. I wish I could make you see that.'

Rocco signalled to the waitress that they were finished
with their starter, keeping his eyes rigidly glued to her
earnest face.

'We're not back to this, are we?'

'The only reason we're here,' Amy pointed out, 'is *because* of this, so how do you expect me to just put it to
one side and pretend that it doesn't exist?'

'Life isn't exclusively about work,' Rocco heard himself say, and he had to muse ironically to himself that he
was a fine one to talk. He did nothing but work. It was
his lifeblood. However, he did not expect to sit having
dinner, and a very good dinner at that, in the company of
a woman and converse about nothing but work. The mere
fact that that was all she was interested in perversely made
him want to veer off the topic completely and corner her
into talking about her hobbies, her past, her personal life.
Anything and everything that did not involve the do-
gooding nonsense she did for a living.

He supposed, though, that she would have to be
dragged kicking and screaming away from the subject.
There was nothing more relentless than a feminist in possession of a cause.

'I'm surprised to hear that coming from you,' Amy said
with asperity, 'considering your life is a testimony to
work.'

'More sweeping assumptions?' With some surprise, he
noticed the waitress who had approached with their main
course. Already? Fish for her and steak in port for him.
He barely noticed the smiling girl putting it in front of
him and didn't focus on her at all as she went through

her well-rehearsed routine speech about hoping that they enjoyed their meals.

Amy dug into her fish. Not only did she and Sam rarely venture into the city centre for a meal, they never indulged in meals like this. Sam simply couldn't afford it on his salary and Amy would never have dreamed of insulting his masculine pride by offering to pay. In fact, Sam would probably have had a heart attack if he knew how much more she earned than him. He had always assumed that they were more or less on equal pay, little realising that the government was a far more stingy employer than Antonio.

'How else could you have gone as far as you have in the space of ten short years if you hadn't devoted every waking moment to your career?' Amy asked reasonably. 'I've read it all.'

Rocco, in the middle of raising his fork to his mouth, stopped and frowned at her, bemused by the remark.

'You've *read it all?*' Rocco's eyebrows shot up. 'Does your work involve you taking out subscriptions to *The New York Times*? Just in case there's some down-and-out community on the other side of the Atlantic in urgent need of funding?'

'*I* wouldn't dream of taking out a subscription to *The New York Times*.' Amy scooped some food onto her fork. Fish that melted in the mouth, vegetables done this side of perfection, a tiny new potato. 'But your father did. He's collected every article ever written about you from the day you went abroad to live and he's shown them all to me.' She lowered her eyes, concentrating on her food and thinking back to Antonio and the pride he took as he measured his son's progress in New York, because Rocco, with his fabulous looks and shadowed background and breathtaking talent for spinning everything he touched into gold, had reached the financial pages very quickly indeed. He was a man who had not been born to go through life unnoticed.

'Would you mind repeating that?'

There was a stillness about him when Amy looked up that made her wonder uneasily what she had said that could have been so offensive.

'I said your father collected articles about you.'

'Is this another psychological ploy to get me feeling guilty about leaving England?' Rocco said harshly, but he was shaken by what she had just confessed. And he knew that she hadn't been lying. She had made the remark too naturally.

'You are the most cynical man I have ever met in my entire life. I can show you where he kept the articles. In fact, I'll tell you. In his library. Bottom drawer of his desk. All neatly stacked in chronological order. Satisfied?'

'If your game is to try and play Chief Liaison Officer between my father and myself in the expectation that you might work a small miracle and thereby secure your career through my gratitude, then you can forget it,' Rocco informed her, resuming his eating. He was disturbed to find that her revelation had got him thinking, though. Why had the old man kept news of him? In the four times during which they had met, only because of certain things that had needed signing to do with his father's company, their conversations had been brief and the barriers that had always existed between them had been as high as they ever had been. He had certainly not got the impression of a father proud of his son's achievements. But then, why the stored articles...? Did those include the gossip column ones as well? Rocco wondered. Now *that* he might understand, if only because they would prove that Antonio had given birth to a son who was adept at making money but unequal to the task of commitment, a fact that the old man had made clear on the few occasions they had met. As Rocco had grown older, he could very well have replied that commitment really wasn't all it was cracked up to be. To commit was to open yourself up to pain. After all, hadn't that been his father's fate? Committed to his wife. So committed, in fact, that when she'd died in childbirth he had found it impossible to move on, impossible even to accept the child she had produced for him.

'The only way I would ever want to secure my career,' Amy said coldly, 'is by proving to you that what we do is, in its own way, invaluable. Whether you and your father make amends is not my concern.' As if to stress just how unconcerned she was, Amy shrugged and closed her knife and fork.

'In fact,' Rocco mused lazily, sitting back in his chair so that he could give her the full benefit of his attention, 'nothing much *is* your concern, is it, aside from holding down your job? Have you ever not felt the desire to pack it in and try your hand at something completely different?'

Amy didn't know which of the two uninvited questions she wanted to respond to first so she looked at him blankly until he shook his head in apparent irritation.

'There is no need to look so disconcerted simply because we have strayed off the topic of the disfranchised and what you can do to help them. Surely you have some experience in making small talk?'

Rocco watched her face redden, either in confusion at his remark or else because she had taken affront at what he had said. Either way, it was a curiously intriguing response. His experiences with women had left him with the jaded feeling that they were really a very predictable species. Particularly the women he had wined, dined and inevitably bedded in New York were aggressively charming, self-confident and never backward at coming forward with details of themselves. They lapped up any questions about themselves as indications of devoted interest. Indeed, falling as they all did into the category of 'Beautiful', they always expected him to be interested in them. They were all women adept at playing the flirting game, enjoying the anticipation of ending up in his bed.

And once they had slept with him, they inevitably moved into phase two of the game, that cosy phase when they attempted to woo him with home-cooked food, preferably cooked in his own gleaming kitchen, proof of their wifely potential, at which point his restlessness would begin to kick in, however sexually alluring the woman in question happened to be.

The girl now staring at him warily was the human equivalent of a brick wall, he decided irritably. Loquacious when it came to spouting forth about charitable causes but aggravatingly uncooperative when it came to discussing anything about herself.

'I'm not disconcerted,' Amy said tightly, 'and I do happen to know what small talk is. In fact, I *thought* that's what we had been making all evening.'

'Would you like some coffee?'

'I think we ought to be getting back.'

'Actually, perhaps a glass of port would be nice. A typically English thing that I must say I have rather missed over the years. Late dinners followed by port and conversation. Americans tend to eat so much earlier than their European counterparts. Join me?' He realised that he had barely touched any of the wine. He must have been more engrossed with the earnest preachings of the charity worker than he had thought. One glass of port certainly wouldn't tip him over the balance.

'I'm amazed you want to prolong the experience of

being here with me,' Amy remarked, still stinging from his implication that she was somehow a social misfit whose only focus in life was her job. 'Considering I can't make small talk.' Now she sounded churlish and sulky, like a reprimanded child. Not the calm, efficient adult who was desperately trying to woo his interest in her cause. 'I've never had port in my life,' she said recklessly, 'but yes, I would love to try a glass.'

'Didn't you ever *want* to come back to England?' Amy heard herself saying, three sips of port later when her head was pleasantly beginning to swim a little. 'I mean,' she elaborated, frowning in concentration and dreadfully aware of those piercing blue eyes staring at her, 'even if you didn't want to have anything to do with Antonio, didn't you ever *miss* life over here? Glasses of port and after-dinner conversation? Pots of tea and scones? The Queen, for heaven's sake!'

The corners of Rocco's mouth twitched and he grinned, which distracted her into gulping down another large mouthful of port. 'The port, yes. Even when I left at twenty-two, I had begun to enjoy it, but port, believe it or not, is not limited to the United Kingdom. Pots of tea and scones, decidedly. Somehow a cup of tea anywhere else in the world never quite tastes the same, would you not agree?'

'I might if I had been to anywhere else in the world.' Amy blushed, feeling gauche and frivolous in equal measure and not at all like the sober-minded girl she was accustomed to.

'As for the Queen,' Rocco drawled, 'I never did manage to make her acquaintance, although I do recall standing outside my school when I was a kid waving a flag as she drove past. Sadly, that did not eventually transpire to an invitation to tea at the palace.'

Amy found herself smiling, captive to his dry humour.

'To answer your question seriously, to begin with, yes…I missed England. It was the only home I ever really knew. Italy was simply somewhere for long holidays. But returning then was not an option.' He swirled his glass between his fingers and then sipped some of the port, looking at her over the rim of the glass. 'Later, I discovered that time had done its thing and New York had gradually filled the void.'

'And you never looked back? With nostalgia?'

'Looking back is a pointless indulgence. The past cannot be changed and therefore it is useless to view it through misty rose-tinted spectacles.'

'Oh.' No wonder he had never made the slightest effort to reopen the lines of communication with his father. For him, Antonio would have been relegated to the past and, as such, to history. And proud Antonio would never have thought of trying to do battle with those sentiments.

'You don't agree, I take it.' For one exasperating moment, he wondered why he was bothering to pursue a discussion that hardly mattered in the big picture.

'I look back all the time,' Amy confessed frankly. 'I think it's good not to let go of your past.'

'Depends on what memories of your past you happen to have.' Rocco's voice was curt. They had both finished their glasses of port, and although it was on the tip of his tongue to order another, maybe because he could sense her itching to escape his company, he didn't. Driving over the limit was never a good idea. 'And don't even think of giving me one of those speciality sympathetic looks of yours. If you didn't spend all your time looking back into the past, don't you think you would be doing something different now?'

'Different like what?'

The bill had been paid and as they stood up she realised that she was just a little reluctant to go. She could only put that down to the fact that she had not managed to persuade him over to her side, which, after all, had been the primary purpose of the evening.

'You tell me. Surely social work wasn't something you yearned to do ever since you were a little girl.'

'It isn't *social work*,' Amy denied vigorously, head held high as they walked through the door, although her brain still felt nicely fuddled and her legs were a little on the unsteady side. 'And I grew into the job.'

'But what if you hadn't had to leave school at sixteen? What would you have done then?' He opened the passenger door for her, a small courtesy that surprised her because it was so old-fashioned in this day and age.

Amy waited until he was in the car before answering. 'I have no idea and, anyway, what's the point of wondering something like that? Do you remember how to get back to my house?'

'More or less.' It was a lot quieter on the roads now and Rocco was surprised to find that it was after midnight. 'Does working on these little projects of yours fulfil some unspoken need in you to be a carer? Having looked after your father, do you think that you simply conditioned yourself into putting other people and their lives ahead of yours?'

'That's absolute rubbish,' Amy answered uneasily.

'Maybe you got so accustomed to not having much light-hearted fun when you were growing up that it seemed natural to drift into the sort of job that you eventually ended up doing,' Rocco persisted, musingly.

'My job is fun!' Amy objected hotly. 'I love doing what I do and don't think that you can brainwash me into thinking that it's a boring waste of time just because that happens to be what *you* think!'

'I think that less after tonight,' he surprised her by saying, but before she could capitalise on the admission he carried on, 'not that I've had any change of heart. It's still a massive waste of talented resources.'

'And now we're talented,' she remarked, her eyes seeking out his perfectly chiselled profile and then remaining there. 'Well, I suppose that's an advance of sorts.' She broke off her mesmerised inspection of his face to give him succinct directions to her street and then kept her eyes firmly averted from him, edgily aware that staring at him could become a very unhealthy habit.

'How did you manage to put your team together?' Rocco asked conversationally.

'Usual way. Interviews.'

'*You* conducted the interviews?'

'Shocking, wouldn't you agree? Little old me, without any qualifications and with only a handful of years' worth of working experience behind me.'

'Which just goes to show what you are capable of doing,' Rocco mused. 'Would you consider coming to New York to work?'

'What?'

'New York. My company could do with a member of staff like you. Competent, willing to take risks, inherently clever and none of those feminine frills that can so easily disturb the balance of a working environment.'

Amy, having recovered from her initial surprise and, she had to admit, pleasure at his suggestion, now focused exclusively on the latter part of his description. *No feminine frills.* She knew what that meant all right. It meant that she was plain enough never to be seen by any man in any working arena as anything less than a competent colleague. She would never be a distraction because she just didn't have what it took to distract.

Amy blinked rapidly as tears of hurt threatened and masked it under a carefully amused laugh.

'I can't think of anything worse,' she informed him, adding silently to herself *than working for an unfeeling, undiplomatic, insulting bastard like you*. How he had ever managed to make her feel *frivolous* of all things, was beyond her. Just the thought that he might have caught her staring at him, as she knew she had done during that meal, was enough to make her cringe with embarrassment. 'I am perfectly happy here, doing what I do…'

'Which may well be about to come to an untimely end.'

'In which case, I shall simply do something else, something that *I* consider worthwhile, something that has nothing to do with the thankless pursuit of stockpiling money.'

'How noble. And what would that something be?'

'I have no idea. I could always return to formal education, get my A levels and then get a degree, go into teacher training…'

They had reached the house before he could start asking too many awkward questions about this idea, though, now she began thinking about it, Amy realised that it was something she really would like to do, should her job collapse. Or when, judging from his relentless zeal to bulldoze them over.

'Thanks for the dinner.' She pushed open the car door and was taken aback to see him follow suit. More taken aback when he followed her to the front door.

'I do have the odd gentlemanly bone in my body,' he said, obviously reading her thoughts as she fumbled in her bag for the front-door key. As if to emphasise the point, he took the key from her fingers before she had time to take the necessary blocking action, and before she knew it he was pushing open the door, allowing her to step inside, allowing her to brush against him, which sent an unnerving feathering of dangerous sensation racing along her spine.

Then, to her dismay, he followed her into the small hallway until she was eventually forced to say, brightly, 'You know your way back to…to your father's house?' Amy hovered, a nervous tension building up inside her like a groundswell.

'I thought I might have a cup of coffee before I begin the long trek back. Have a fifteen-minute break before I begin the journey.'

'It shouldn't take you long to get there,' she dodged. 'There won't be any traffic at all on the roads at this time…' This was greeted with unnerving silence until she cleared her throat and got a grip of her thundering heart. 'Of course, if you feel you *need* a cup of coffee, then sure…'

He did. Especially when he saw how reluctant she was to provide it. A cup of coffee in the confines of her house was probably way beyond the call of duty. Her brief was to convert him to her way of thinking and anything beyond that, such as a simple courteous gesture, was not within the specified parameters.

Rocco looked around and pointedly shut the door behind him. Her house was small but cosy. No frills and nothing fussy, but he could tell from the pictures on the walls and the renovated pieces of furniture that everything had been bought carefully and with love.

Sensing that she was watching him, he finally turned back to her.

'The sitting room's through there.' Amy indicated a door to his right. 'If you want to wait there I'll bring you a cup of coffee.'

'It's no bother, is it?' he asked innocently.

'Why should it be? Anyway, you've just taken me out for a splendid meal…'

She turned on her heel and disappeared in the direction of the kitchen, leaving him to make his way to the small sitting room and ponder the unappreciated novelty of having the shoe on the other foot for the first time. He had been through enough times with women when they insisted on staying on, incapable of sensing his restlessness for them to leave.

He could hear the distant noises of rustling in the kitchen as she reluctantly made the coffee he had insisted he needed, and was asking himself what he had to gain by being here when he could be driving back to his house when the telephone rang.

The telephone right next to him.

It was an automatic gesture to pick it up and answer it although he had only managed one sentence when she flew into the lounge just as he was replacing the receiver.

'Did I just hear the phone?'

'You did.'

Amy looked at the phone, now resting inert in its cradle. 'Why didn't you call me?'

'And disturb you in the middle of your coffee-making exercise?' The joke fell as flat as a lead balloon and gut reaction told him that the last thing he wanted to do was show any sign of amusement, although she presented a very amusing picture indeed, standing there with her hands on her hips, glaring at him, red in the face. 'It was your boyfriend,' Rocco informed her, 'and I would have called you but I automatically picked it up because it was right next to me.'

'Sam? It was Sam?'

'I did offer to go and get you but he said not to bother, that he'd call you in the morning.'

Amy walked into the sitting room and groaned.

'You had no right to…to pick the phone up!' she snapped belatedly.

'What is the problem?'

'The problem?' She stalked further into the room, wondering how poor Sam would have reacted to the sound of that deep, lazy drawl down the end of the line at this ungodly hour of the night. 'The *problem* is that you answered the phone! That's the problem! I'd better phone him and explain. No. Better not. If I rush in immediately, I'll sound guilty. Of course I'm *not* guilty, but I'll *sound* guilty. Arghhh…' She sat down on one of the chairs and glared at the uninvited sex god on the sofa. Typical. Cool as a cucumber when the whole thing was his fault!

CHAPTER FIVE

ROCCO left Amy with her thoughts while he went into the kitchen, rescued his mug of coffee from the counter and made her one.

Taste. The woman had taste as well. Not only was the décor a testimony to the pride she obviously took in her surroundings, it was also a testimony to taste. He had always assumed that raging feminists had no taste. Something to do with his belief that their every waking moment was spent furiously chasing boring causes with yawn-inducing fervour. But the kitchen was charming. Bright yellow walls adorned with small posters of quirky pop art in clip frames, green wooden shutters at the window instead of curtains to match the units, which had been hand-painted, and a small kitchen table that was pale and smooth and clearly budget, but tasteful budget.

He returned to the sitting room to find that she hadn't budged.

'Coffee.'

'What?'

'Coffee. Strong. You look as though you need it, although what the problem is is beyond me.' He moved back to the sofa, sat down, sipped from his mug and proceeded to look at her.

'There's no *problem*,' Amy said irritably, glancing across at him and feeling that he had somehow made yet more inroads into her personal life by going into her kitchen and making her some coffee. A perfectly innocuous gesture that countless people had done over the course of time, including all the men working with her and who had been visitors to her house over the years.

'I would say that your reaction to Sam—it *is* Sam, isn't it?—hearing my voice down the end of the line is a bit on the hysterical side. He *did* know that we would be spending the evening together, didn't he?'

'Of course he knew that we would be…would be spending the evening together.' Amy stumbled over the words, which were literally accurate but unfortunately a bit too provocative for her liking. 'On business,' she added. 'In fact, he thought that it was a brilliant idea for you to come along with me to have a look at our project.'

'Well…there you go…'

'I'm just not sure that he expected us to end up having dinner together.'

'You make it sound as though we ended up in bed together…' Rocco's lazy blue eyes bored into her and he finally gave shape to the nebulous feeling that had been plaguing him. Bed. Him. Her. He had watched her as she'd performed with enthusiasm and conviction in that room this evening, had seen the way she interacted with all those people, dealing with them in just the right way, with respect and willingness to listen to what they had to say. And the sheer novelty of her had sent his imagination soaring.

Maybe, he thought, his imagination had been soaring even before then. She certainly was nothing like any woman he had come into contact with before and didn't most red-blooded males get excited at the thought of a challenge?

He battened down his imagination and reminded himself that work and play didn't mix. In fact, it was a rule of his never to get involved with someone from work, and this particular woman was virtually falling off the scale when it came to unsuitability, not least because he was her boss, so to speak, and a boss with a duty to get rid of her.

'Don't be ridiculous!' she snapped, bringing him right back down to earth with a vengeance. Lord knew how his imagination had managed to slip its reins, he thought irritably, when the woman was as appealing as barbed wire.

'I'm not being ridiculous,' Rocco grated, leaning forward and resting his elbows on his knees, cradling the mug between his long fingers. 'You're behaving like someone who has been caught out. If the man trusted you, it wouldn't occur to him that my answering the telephone implied anything suspicious.'

'Of course Sam trusts me!' She had a sinking feeling that whatever conversation she had with him the following day would be an uphill battle against his querulous petulance and questions bordering on accusations. All his self-righteous fervour would stampede to the fore at the thought of her entertaining a Man Like Him.

'But how would you feel if you telephoned your girlfriend at this hour of the night and the phone was answered by a strange man?'

'But I'm not a strange man.'

'You know what I mean!'

Rocco shrugged and continued to look at her, which was something she definitely didn't want. He was too damned sexy and she knew that if he had been fat, bald, unappealing, she wouldn't have felt a twinge of guilt at having him under her roof, drinking her coffee, at an hour when she should be curled up in bed fast asleep.

'Okay. I get your point. I suppose if I had called a girlfriend at night and a man had picked up the phone, I might have been a little curious as to what he was doing there, but—' at this point, Rocco shrugged with utter honesty '—all's fair in love and war. If my woman was two-timing me then I would drop her faster than a hot potato.'

'Just like that.' Amy, distracted from the thought of a questioning, accusatory Sam, looked right back at Rocco. She could feel that curiosity again, the biting curiosity to know *about him*, a curiosity that had nothing to do with winning him over to her cause or making him see the importance of what she and her team did in the bigger picture.

'Just like that,' Rocco drawled, snapping his fingers to emphasise his point.

'And you…you wouldn't feel…well…*bad?*'

'Bad? Why would I feel bad?'

'Because relationships make you sensitive to the other person's feelings? Because it would hurt to think that someone was behaving badly behind your back? Because you would have invested time and emotion in getting to know someone only to discover that you hadn't really known them after all?'

'No to all those things,' he said. Another personal conversation. The woman had an unfortunate knack of dragging him into them without him even realising. When she didn't answer, he shook his head and frowned accusingly at her. 'And you can stop looking at me as if I were a pitiful wretch. I just don't allow myself to get involved to such a point that I can't walk away.'

'That's probably why you just don't understand how emotionally involved I am with what I do,' Amy pointed out. She was staring again. At least they were conversing so she had a reason to look at him, she thought. At least she wasn't just staring witlessly as she had done at dinner, observing his face, the strength of his features, the sensuous curve of his mouth, the harsh beauty of his bone structure. Ruthless, cruel men should repel. They shouldn't fascinate. Good, caring men like Sam should fascinate.

'Oh, not here again.'

The groan that came from him was enough to make her smile. 'Are you trying to tell me that I'm repetitive?'

Rocco looked at the teasing lilt of her mouth. She had done clever things with the lighting, the sort of things he always did with his. Avoided the overhead light, relied instead on the dimmer, more mellow lighting given off from lamps, one of them a standing light that could be controlled. It gave the room a soft atmosphere conducive to relaxing and talking. And looking. He found his thoughts wandering off to the so-called boyfriend that had caused such a disturbance and found himself tensing.

'Not to mention relentless,' he said roughly. 'Do you ever climb down from the soapbox?'

'That's not very nice.'

'I am not a very nice person.'

'I realise that.' The smile became a grin. She realised that thoughts of a disgruntled Sam had vanished from her head like a puff of smoke.

'Many thanks for that,' Rocco said sarcastically but with good humour crinkling the corners of his eyes. The coffee was finished but still he delayed stirring himself and getting a move on. He also realised, with delayed surprise, that she had just insulted him. In a manner of speaking. And the feeling that had given him was nothing like the one he would have expected.

'I have to go,' he said abruptly, leaning so that he could deposit the empty mug on the table in front of him, a low, square smooth table like the one in the kitchen, budget but tasteful budget.

'Of course.' Amy stood up as well with a feeling of disappointment.

'Good luck for tomorrow.'

'For tomorrow? Why? What's happening tomorrow?'

'Your awkward conversation with your boyfriend.' He moved towards the door of the sitting room, following her out into the hallway.

'Oh, right. Yes. Thank you. You were right. I was getting a bit manic over nothing. Sam knows me well enough to know that I'd never do anything, especially with you.'

'With me?' Rocco, *en route* to the front door, stopped in his tracks to look down at her.

Amy blushed. 'Well. He knows that you want to get rid of us…'

'I don't want to *get rid of you*,' Rocco said harshly. 'I already told you that my father's company could use people like you, like all of you. We've been through all of this…'

'Anyway, he knows that I would never…never…' The confident riposte died on her lips and she struggled to find the right words to express thoughts that would have been better kept in her head.

'Never…what?' As if to forestall the option of her flinging the door open and allowing the conversation to disappear into the night air, Rocco planted himself very firmly against it and folded his arms.

A delicate, guilty flush had crept into her cheeks.

'Never…you know…'

'Nope. Haven't got a clue.'

'You know exactly what I mean, Rocco!' When he continued to look at her with that patient, baffled expression, she sighed impatiently. 'Sam knows that I would never *do anything with you*. He knows that you're not the kind of man I could ever be interested in *in that way*. So thank you for your concern, but there won't be any jealous scenes tomorrow, believe me.'

'Beware the man who is never jealous,' Rocco drawled. 'It's a primitive emotion but then so is possessiveness. A man in love is a jealous man. He is also a possessive man.'

'In this day and age?' Amy laughed nervously. He dwarfed the small hall, just as he had dwarfed the small sitting room. Or maybe his personality was so strong that the minute he was in any room he gave the impression of taking over. 'Women aren't into jealousy and possessiveness.' She imagined the big, powerful man in front of her following his woman's movements with his eyes, staking his claim, and pushed the mad thought out of her head. Those were despicable characteristics and always ended in tears. Weren't control freaks jealous, possessive types?

'Besides, from what you've said you've never been jealous of anyone...' She found that she was a little breathless and wished that she had never conceived the crazy idea of avoiding bright lights in the house, opting for dimmer switches that were permanently turned down low. True it went a long way to concealing anything unfortunate that might be happening to the wallpaper, but the downside was this. Standing here, with this man towering above her and the subdued, mellow lighting making her feel ridiculously light-headed and giddy. There was an awful lot to be said for fluorescent lighting.

'Like I said, jealousy is a natural, healthy by-product of being in love. Something I have avoided to date...'

Shouldn't they be discussing pressing business?

She heard herself saying, defensively, 'Well, Sam... loves me...and he's not the jealous type...'

Rocco's eyebrows raised in amused disbelief. Well, Amy thought with sudden anger, he had been pretty surprised to hear that she could manage to find a boyfriend, no wonder he was incredulous at the thought that said boyfriend might actually love her.

'In fact, he's asked me to marry him!'

This was greeted by stupendous silence. Rocco, staring down at the hot and bothered face with its *so there* expression, felt suddenly winded. As if he had been punched unexpectedly in the gut when he hadn't been looking. It was such a shocking reaction for him that it took a few seconds to recover.

'Should I be offering my congratulations?' he asked lazily.

Amy didn't say anything, eager to terminate the conversation at this point before further delving into this area of her personal life began.

'Because,' he continued remorselessly, 'you haven't mentioned whether you have accepted or not.'

'Naturally, marriage is a huge deal. A girl needs to consider lots of…*angles*…before reaching any kind of decision.'

'Naturally,' Rocco murmured.

'Which Sam fully understands.'

'I'm sure.' He lounged against the closed door and folded his arms.

'Gosh!' Registering this slight alteration in his stance, which seemed to indicate no hurry to leave, Amy gave a high laugh and smiled brightly. 'How boring for you, listening to all this private nonsense from me!' She peered to see whether the handle of the door was available so that she could add further pointed emphasis to her dismissive, cheerful exclamation by meaningfully putting her hand on it. No such luck. He was resolutely barricading the exit. The only way to get past him would be to shove him forcibly out of the way and there was no chance of that happening considering he was over six foot and in possession of an off-puttingly muscular body.

'As I have told you before, hearing about the personal lives of my employees makes them three—'

'Dimensional…yes, you *have* told me before.'

'Might solve your dilemma, though,' Rocco mused thoughtfully, stroking his chin with one finger as if giving his thoughts a great deal of consideration.

'Oh, yes?'

'A married woman is a woman who begins nest-building, and nest-building doesn't usually go hand in hand with a demanding career.'

The sheer masculine, outdated arrogance of that statement brought a high gasp of outraged protest to her lips.

'Unless, of course, your Sam is one of those forward-thinking men who encourage their women to carry on working after the "I do's" have been uttered…?' Rocco offered into the momentarily stunned silence.

Amy had a swift and unpleasant reminder of what she had felt when Sam had made his proposition. His vague assurances that she could give up her job and take up something a lot less stressful, thereby saving herself for his needs.

'Sam isn't *my* man,' was all she could find to say to his sweeping observation. 'And your problems aren't going to be solved by me conveniently getting married and settling down to wash clothes and iron until the pitter patter of tiny feet arrive! Anyway, you've forgotten that it isn't just *my* job hanging in the balance. There are also five other hard-working people involved!'

'With whom I would like to have a meeting some time soon, now that you mention it.'

'Why?' Amy threw at him, still uncomfortable at the image that Rocco had managed to portray of Sam without actually meaning to. 'Will what you have to say to them be any different than what you have to say to me? They already know what your long-range plans are. That appealing to your heart as opposed to your head doesn't stand a chance of working because you *have* no emotions and you *have* no heart.'

'Is that a fact?'

The low, amused voice brought her thundering heart to a sudden standstill before sending it soaring to a faster beat.

'Yes,' she virtually squeaked. 'You know it is! You said it yourself so you can't turn around and accuse me of nosing into your precious private life! You don't get emotionally involved with women and you refuse to get emotionally involved with what we do! You see everything in black and white and you just dismiss all the grey areas in between!'

He must be getting used to her unique way of addressing him without any thought of the consequences, he realised grimly, just as she didn't give any passing notice to trying to make an impression, because he didn't bat an eyelid at her outburst.

In fact, he didn't give much thought to anything. He reacted purely on gut response, which was why he reached out one hand, cupped the nape of her neck and pulled her towards him.

She hadn't been expecting that, Rocco thought with a surge of pure, red-blooded, male satisfaction. Her eyes widened and up close now he could even see her pupils dilate, but before her brain could make the necessary connections, and with a groan of having finally got his hands on something he had been wanting for a while, he lowered his head so that he could prove to her just how wrong she was about him being cold and unfeeling.

In the split second before his mouth hit hers she knew what he was going to do, and then for a brief, terrifying while she was lost and drowning as his warm lips found her parted, startled ones and his tongue probed against hers. His hand moved sensuously against her neck and she unconsciously curved towards him, liking this drowning feeling, wanting more of it.

Pressed up against him, her breasts were crushed against the hard breadth of his chest and her nipples stiffened and ached at the contact. She could lose herself in this. It was bigger and more overwhelming than anything she had ever experienced in her life before. As if floodgates had suddenly been flung open, allowing a tidal rush of sensation she had never known existed before to pelt through her system.

It was wonderful, it was utterly consuming and it was…wrong.

Reality suddenly doused her and she pushed herself away from him, finding herself released immediately.

'What do you think you're *doing?*' Her voice was unsteady and her hands were trembling. In fact, she seemed to be trembling all over, like someone in the grip of fever-induced ague.

The reaction did not escape Rocco's notice and he derived savage pleasure from it. Indeed, he was tempted to throw the question right back at her, but he allowed her her moral outrage while a million questions zinged in his head. Such as how she could be contemplating marrying someone when her response to him was as dramatic as that, short-lived though it had been.

The raging feminist, he thought to himself, was brimming over with fire and that brief glimpse of the fire had left him with a painfully stiff arousal, which he concealed by pushing himself away from the door and then opening it so that the cool night air could do something helpful.

'I thought that was obvious.' His mouth was oddly dry and he couldn't quite meet her eyes, unusual for him, because he knew that if he did the surge of response would do nothing to release his aching groin.

Mortification raged through her like a forest fire. *Proving a point.* That was what he had been doing and, as far as he was concerned, it should have been as obvious to her as it was to him. She had called him cold, unfeeling, incapable of emotion and he had responded brutally to prove her wrong. What was mortifying was that she had enjoyed it. Instead of shoving him off her the minute he'd touched her, she had idiotically gone into a kind of weird state of suspended animation that had allowed her to respond. And there was no justifying that.

'You don't like argument, do you?' she seethed, giving full vent to her self-disgust by attacking. 'You don't like being criticised and that was your way of dealing with it!'

This time he did meet her eyes, on the way out of the house, one foot already on the doorstep. A sharp gust of wind blew his hair and he impatiently raked his fingers through it. 'Maybe. But what was *your* reason for kissing me back?'

'I think it's time you left.'

'Consider this: how strong is the relationship with your fiancé-to-be if another man can fire you up the way I just did?'

'You…you took me by surprise, that's all,' she spluttered, red-faced.

'Fine.' Rocco shrugged, annoyed because, when he thought about it, *she* had taken him by surprise as well. And he had surprised himself just by how gratifying that kiss had been. If she hadn't come to her senses and pushed him away, he would have carried right on kissing her and then more. His response had been a hell of a lot more than just teaching her a lesson in curbing her sharp tongue.

He almost laughed as he strode towards his car. Rocco Losi, the biggest cat in the New York jungle, a man legendary for his liaisons with women who could grace the cover of *Vogue* any time they chose, and some of them had, sharing a three-second kiss with a stubborn, opinionated slip of a girl and feeling like an adolescent whose closest brush with a naked woman was in the centre pages of a girlie magazine.

'By the way,' he called, half turning as she was about to firmly close the door, 'don't forget about that meeting. The one I want to arrange with all the members of your team. I'll get the secretary to telephone you tomorrow to fix up an appropriate date.'

At which point Amy slammed the door. Her lips still stung from that kiss and her body was only now beginning feel like her body instead of candlewax that had undergone a process of meltdown, and there he was, calmly focusing on work, probably already planning out what was lined up for the day ahead.

But then proving a point didn't have any lasting side effects.

By the time she had crawled under the covers half an hour later, she had convinced herself that she would be a side-effect-free zone as well, and, despite her misgivings, she managed to sink into a blissful, dreamless sleep for the next six hours.

She only wished it could have been a little bit longer when she was abruptly dragged to consciousness by the phone ringing by her bed at six-fifteen. It was Sam. Her head was so full of pictures of the odious Rocco that it took her a few seconds to switch the connections and focus on the man asking her down the end of the line how things had gone with the big, bad wolf and whether she could meet up with him later, after work.

'I *was* going to try and get you later today on your mobile, but I'm on a one-day course and you know what those things are like.'

Yes, she did. Dull affairs with mediocre finger foods for lunch, which Sam would eat with gusto, while basking in the enjoyment of being surrounded by dozens of fellow colleagues with the same blinkered intolerance that he had.

Amy, dismayed by that rush of uncharitable feeling, sat up and took a more focused interest in what he was saying, agreeing to meet him at seven at their usual pizza place, even though she would have preferred to catch up on her paperwork.

She kept expecting him to launch into her for Rocco's presence in her house after the witching hour, but he didn't. He was tetchy on the point of her asking him back to the house for coffee but then explained it away without intervention from her by saying that he understood, if that was what was needed to persuade him into changing his mind, while quickly reminding her that it really wasn't the end of the world if he didn't.

By the time she hung up, she was wide awake and oddly deflated by the phone call.

'Fits of jealousy,' she told herself as she got ready for work, '*bad*. Calm and soothing trust…*good*.' She repeated it at frequent intervals to herself throughout the course of the day and was only jogged out of the mantra and the glum feeling that went with it when, at four-thirty, the telephone rang on her desk and a sexy, low drawl made her heartbeat begin to race.

The man who kissed to prove a point.

The man who wanted a meeting with the team so that he could tell them what he had already told her.

'I'm busy for the remainder of the week,' he informed her and she had a very graphic image of him sitting back in the chair, his brilliant eyes half looking at a computer screen while his brilliant mind half listened to her.

'Then it'll have to be next week, won't it?' She flicked through her diary, absent-mindedly registering her own handwriting on the pages and thinking of that wretched kiss that had knocked her for six.

'But I have a free slot this afternoon.'

'*This afternoon?* In case you hadn't checked your watch, the afternoon is already in full swing and about to come to a close.'

'Oh, is it? I should be able to get over to your office by six, once I'm through with some business here.'

'That's…that's a little difficult…' Amy said tactfully, wondering whether Sam's patience would stretch to another cancelled date, then deciding that she had no option but to meet him, whatever. The relationship was going nowhere, yet another one of those, and she would have to tell him because there was no point in stringing him along and giving him time to nurture unrealistic ideas about where they were heading, which was definitely not up an aisle.

'Oh, yes. Enlighten me as to why.'

'Half the team are out and about…'

'Call them on their mobiles, let them know that they have to be at the office by six for a meeting. I should think they'd have been all too happy to oblige considering their futures will be under discussion.'

'Under discussion? Isn't that a bit of an understatement?'

'Let's not get into semantics, Amy. Just call them and tell them I'll be there between six and six-thirty. I'll take you all out to dinner afterwards.'

'To soften the blow?'

'Stop treating me like the enemy,' Rocco grated down the end of the line. Something had happened last night. He wasn't too sure what but he knew that she was already retreating back into the categories she had established and he was damned if he was going to let her do that. On some level, he threatened her safety, and not just the safety of her job, but running away wasn't going to help. In the normal course of things, he was more than happy to let people get on with screwing up their lives. In this instance, though, he felt an irrational desire to personally throttle her into facing facts and working with them. Where, he wondered irritably, had this rogue interfering gene come from? And why was he giving it houseroom when there were a dozen important things to be done, deals to be sewn up via conference calls that would net him substantial sums of money, at least two business trips to plan that would go some way to making his name a global byword?

'Oh, OK. You're right.' Amy capitulated with the sudden, easy grace of someone who had other plans in mind. She would assemble the team and she, herself, would let them get on with it so that she could go and get this meeting with Sam over and done with. It wasn't, after all, as if Rocco Losi would have anything new to say to her. She'd heard it all before and she could sum it up in a few succinct phrases. The man was a money-making machine with a heart of stone who was determined to close their subsidiary, however loudly they protested. And he would do it with a sadistic smile on his face.

'So I will expect you to be there...' He found that he

was looking forward to seeing her and wondered, restlessly, whether her do-gooding tendencies were somehow getting into his system by some cunning process of osmosis. Why else would he give one damn whether he laid eyes on the girl again, were it not for his newly discovered charitable concern that she sort herself out, job, men, the lot?

Amy brushed past the question with alacrity. 'I'll make sure we're well stocked with coffee! Can't say the team is going to be bowled over at the prospect of hanging around for a meeting, but, as you say, it's important for them to hear the cold facts from the horse's mouth rather than second hand from me. Chinese whispers, you know…'

'What are you talking about?'

Good question, Amy thought. She was rambling. His disembodied voice on the telephone was enough to bring her out in a cold sweat. 'Can you give me a definite time for when you'll be arriving? I wouldn't want them to be hanging around until all hours of the night. Marcy has commitments at home. She'll have to arrange a babysitter.'

'No later than six-thirty.'

By which time, Amy was in her house, getting ready to meet Sam. She had gathered her troops together, explained that the Big Boss wanted to see them, which had ignited a round of jeering, assured them that her presence was not essential because she had already heard everything there was to say on the subject of their non-profit-making organisation. Her time, she had confided to her five friends and workmates, would be better spent meeting Sam at the pizza place so that she could break off their relationship.

And that had been the end of any business discussion.

The remaining half an hour had been spent fending off various opinions on Sam and the nature of relationships in general. Those five people, she now thought, staring at her reflection in the mirror, were like family to her. The only family she had, now that Antonio was soon to go to Italy and would be incommunicado except via telephone or e-mail. Was it any wonder that she was so protective about them and so desperate to see that they all kept their jobs? Something Rocco Losi, with his clear-cut, black-and-white image of life, would never understand. The hard, dynamic face superimposed itself over hers in the mirror and she had a moment of deep nervousness as she wondered whether he had arrived at the office and what his reaction would be when he discovered that she wasn't there.

Then more worrying thoughts took over as she contemplated a difficult time ahead with Sam. He had always been the soul of kindness and understanding…but… underneath the kindness was a certain amount of truculence and a sort of pettiness that she had only recently become aware of. Pettiness and truculence, she thought as she stepped out of the house and headed for her car, could be the enemies of a peaceful finale.

Sam was at the pizza place, waiting for her when she arrived after being stuck in traffic for fifteen minutes. Temporary traffic lights had been erected one block away from her house and bollards strategically placed to indicate an area in which no visible work appeared to be taking place. For one disorienting second, Amy was struck by the stark comparison between Sam and Rocco, then she moved towards him, nervously smiling and with a sinking heart.

'You're…' he looked at his watch humorously '…twenty minutes late.'

'Traffic.' She had never noticed how tired this place was before. It had probably possessed a winning formula ten years ago when it had been built, but since then it had been overtaken by fast-food restaurants with even more winning formulas. Now it looked jaded and worn down.

'You look exhausted.' Having stood up to greet her, he subsided back into his chair and looked at her frowningly. 'Guess things are not going quite as you wanted them to with the Italian?'

'His name's Rocco, Sam.' When he beamed at her and winked, as if involving her in a private joke, and then stretched out his hand to cover hers, she tactfully pulled back and tucked both her hands firmly on her lap.

How was she going to get through this? she wondered. He barely seemed to notice that, while he spoke for twenty minutes about his course and the various soul mates he had met there, waving aside the waitress because he was still too wrapped up in his conversation for food, she had scarcely uttered a word.

'Look,' she said, when finally there was a lapse in the monologue. She leant forward, drawing him towards her, and placed her hands over his. 'I've given this a lot of thought, and there's something I need to say to you...'

CHAPTER SIX

Rocco had had no trouble in either locating the pizza place, which was just off the main drag of the high street, or in locating Sam and Amy, mainly because the restaurant was half empty. Two waitresses, who looked young enough to still be in high school, were lounging by the cash register and chatting in a desultory manner, and the rest of the diners, all eight of them, were talking in such low voices that, were it not for the décor, anyone would be forgiven for thinking that they had walked into a slightly odd library.

There was a little flurry of animation by the cash register at his arrival, which he noticed out of the corner of his eye, but by the time the blonder of the two waitresses had surfaced sufficiently to head towards him he was already striding towards the table where its two occupants were conversing with heads close together.

He was just in time to catch the tail-end of Amy's sentence and as the implications of it struck home he was assaulted by such a rage of jealousy that for a split second he was virtually paralysed. Then a lifetime of self-control took over, and he was himself again.

Neither occupant of the table had seen him. They were absorbed in each other. As they would be, he thought acidly, interrupting the loving little scenario by imposing himself between them, hands placed squarely on the small table. Accepting a proposal of marriage, which had been undoubtedly on her lips, required concentration. It wasn't the sort of thing you casually let slip over a mouthful of half-chewed pizza.

'Am I interrupting anything?' Rocco looked lazily between them, and before either could answer he had pulled out a chair and sat down.

Amy was the first to break the thick silence and she realised that, underneath all the anxiousness over her meeting with Sam, she had been worried stiff about what Rocco would do when he discovered her absence from his prearranged meeting. Now she knew.

'What are you doing here? How did you find me?'

'Ever full of questions, isn't she?' Rocco sat back in his chair and turned to look at Sam. Just as he had expected. A man without vigour, a man who had earnest acceptance written all over his face as well as that peculiarly defensive thrust of his jaw that indicated someone who saw himself as having been dealt an unfair blow in life. Rocco had met many like him before. Always vociferous on the Evils of Wealth, never daring to push themselves towards such a target for fear of failing in the process. Complaint and inaction were always so much more comfortable than aiming for the stars.

He turned back towards her, looked at her angry face, noted the speedy removal of her hands from her fiancé's, and felt another burst of dark, incomprehensible emotion that left in its wake a grim determination to yank her back from the abyss she was clearly hurtling towards. Sorting out the personal lives of his employees was not in his job specification, but he would make an exception in this instance and little did she know how grateful she would be in the long run.

'I am Rocco Losi and you must be Sam,' he said, introducing himself but declining the regulatory handshake.

'You still haven't answered my questions.'

'I will in a minute. First, some wine, I think.' He flicked a glance at the waitress, who scurried across breathlessly, smoothing her uniform as she approached, and Rocco ordered a bottle of the house white, ignoring Sam's interjection that he was not a drinker. 'Everyone drinks,' he said with such sweeping arrogance that Amy glared ferociously but fruitlessly at his averted profile. 'Except those who see some virtue in resisting temptation. I have always thought that succumbing to a little temptation is very good for the soul, as a matter of fact.'

'And we're both thrilled to hear that piece of wisdom, but would you mind telling me what you're doing here?' She hadn't even got around to telling Sam what she had to say and her chances now appeared blown to the four winds.

'There was a certain little meeting…?'

'Which was scheduled out of working hours,' Sam interjected huffily. 'Amy is not obliged to work beyond five o'clock in the afternoon. Nine to five. Those are her statutory working hours.'

Rocco glanced at him as though he had suddenly started speaking in tongues and then ignored him.

'I was a little surprised to find you absent, especially when you know my feelings on members of staff who are not prepared to go the full distance.'

Please don't say anything, Sam, she pleaded silently. One more sanctimonious interjection about working hours and she had a gut feeling that Rocco would make mincemeat of him.

'I didn't think you would have anything new to add to the equation,' Amy explained calmly, apologetically, just wanting to get rid of him so that she could bid her farewells to Sam and not have that lingering over her head any longer. 'I didn't think my presence would be missed.'

And of course, Rocco completed to himself, rushing over to start wedding plans was so much more exciting than the so-called fulfilling career she had been harping on about relentlessly ever since she'd found out his intentions. He looked at her coldly.

'Your members of staff might disagree on that.' He watched as her shoulders tensed. 'Which, incidentally, is why they agreed to let me know where I might find you.' The wine had arrived. It tasted awful and drinking on his own while two lovers waited politely for him to leave suddenly seemed very sad somehow.

He had never felt *sad* in his life before, dammit. He was the most bloody fulfilled person he knew. He worked relentlessly, made enough money to keep him in apartments the world over if he so chose, was respected, admired, fawned upon and enjoyed the pleasure of women without the grinding monotony of commitment. He repelled the inner voice that chattered in his head about his relationship with his father, as he did the image of this woman next to him reaching out to hold her lover's hands the minute his back was turned.

He stood up abruptly, pushing the chair back, and looked down at them.

'Maybe you could see your way to getting to my office tomorrow. If you can find a window in your busy personal life.'

'That's unfair!' Amy protested, blushing furiously.

'Amy works considerable hours, Mr Losi,' Sam said, annoyed to be relegated to the sidelines by an intruder. 'Your father has never had a problem with her dedication—'

'I am capable of defending myself, Sam!' There was sharp irritation in her voice, which Rocco picked up on and found quite satisfying, but his face was perfectly bland when he turned to Sam, head inclined to one side, a picture of polite interest.

'Oh, no. I welcome your input…Sam…always interesting to hear viewpoints from a third party…'

'I can be with you first thing in the morning, if that's convenient,' Amy blurted out, desperate to interrupt this unfolding scenario in which Rocco was definitely the stalking predator with eyes firmly fixed on his bewildered, innocent prey.

'Well,' Sam huffed, more than happy to expand on his train of thought, 'I'm certainly very glad to hear that, Mr Losi. All too often, people in your position, and I use the term *people* because women play a powerful role in our society these days, don't feel that they need to hear what the ordinary folk are saying…'

Amy groaned silently to herself while Rocco wore an expression of focused interest highly disproportionate to what the other man was actually saying. If one look could carry a wealth of sarcasm, she thought with hostility, then Rocco Losi had mastered such a look. She didn't know whether to be happy or sad that Sam seemed oblivious to any undercurrent. She listened to him ramble on for a few minutes and lacked the energy to object when, at the end of what seemed an interminable length of time, he gently linked his fingers through hers.

'Amy and I have a lot to discuss,' he finished, smiling complacently at Rocco. 'Hence her uncustomary disregard for work in this instance. Not a habit, I assure you!'

'Right. I'll leave you to it, then, shall I?' Rocco thrust his hands into his pockets and smiled stiffly at them. He had drunk one glass of wine and he nodded curtly at the bottle. 'Sample some of the devil's drink,' he said pointedly to Sam, hands clenched in his pockets. 'You might find you like it.'

'Might just do that.'

Rocco strode off without a backward glance. Let the imbecile commit her folly, he thought, settling into the plush seat of his car and slamming the door behind him. She was young. She would have a good while to repent, and repent she would. He headed away from the city then, when the prospect of a clear journey out to the country awaited him, took the next turning and headed straight back in, to the same area where he and Amy had had dinner.

It was obligingly busy, just what he needed, and even more obligingly full of bars, feet deep in people.

He got himself a small whisky and found a bar stool at the corner, where he sat following his mind down dark, unexplored corners that he sure as hell hadn't visited before. Or, at least, not for a very long time.

His days of uncertainty as far as his relationship with his father was concerned were a thing of the past, an unpleasant memory relegated to adolescence, when private uncertainty had crystallised into a ferocious determination to move on, which he had done with admirable effectiveness. New York had been his salvation. So what was coming back here doing for him? he wondered, shoving one empty glass aside and ordering another.

He had unearthed the scrapbook she had told him about, and had found himself stored in its pages. His history was all there, as his name in New York had grown in status. Events that he could scarcely remember, affairs when the press had been around, snapping pictures for gossip columns, had been chronicled and carefully stuck in the pages of an impressive hard-covered tome. He had seen himself at the age of seven, dressed in his little uniform, bags at his side, ready to face the big, bad world of boarding-school. God, he couldn't even remember who had taken that one!

He had barely communicated with his father since he'd been back in England. Just the bare bones of conversations, when practicalities had been discussed. More often than not, someone else had been present.

By the time he had downed his third whisky, he realised that driving back was not going to be an option. He would have to leave his car in the car park overnight and have it delivered back to him in the morning.

And the thought of going back to the house wasn't too great a prospect either. He'd had enough of this particular little trip down memory lane. He needed company. Unfortunately, his social life appeared to have been temporarily left in America. If he had been there, there would have been innumerable people he could have called on, not to mention a number of women who would have been more than delighted to have scrambled to his summons and relieved him of the tedium of his thoughts.

Here, though, his social life was a matter of necessity, functions that he had attended through duty and a distinct absence of the opposite sex.

Between getting a taxi and contemplating an empty house waiting for him, the idea of paying a little visit to Amy came to him almost out of nowhere, then the more he thought about it, the better an idea it appeared to be.

Why, he had no idea, but he didn't stop to question that. His brain was not up to par at the moment. Asking it too many detailed questions didn't seem such a good idea. He just gave the taxi driver her address, sat back and enjoyed the lack of scenery.

Half an hour later, Amy heard the banging on her front door and emitted a long groan of despair.

The past hour and a half had been the longest of her life.

How had she ever imagined that Sam was the soul of placidity?

As soon as Rocco had left the table, he had settled in with a satisfied smile, eager to hear what he felt certain had been coming, namely an acceptance of his marriage proposal.

As she had quietly explained that she wasn't going to get engaged, never mind get married, the smile had faded from his face to give way to an expression of disbelief.

'But I-I don't understand…' he had stammered, which had made her feel terrible. 'We get along so well. You would be the first to say how well we get along!'

'Yes, but…'

Her 'yes, buts' had increased with each objection he had raised. They understood each other's fields of work…*yes, but*…they had similar aspirations in life, or so he had always imagined…*yes, but*…neither of them smoked or even really drank…*yes, but*…until, finally, she had been forced to be utterly uncompromising. She simply was not in love with him, at which point things had taken a definite turn downwards.

Bewilderment had given way to self-righteous anger as, face mottled and thrust towards her, he had accused her of leading him on, of giving him false impressions, of taking advantage of his good nature. In stunned silence, she had listened to the ugly face of rejection and had eventually walked out of the restaurant when his accusations had spiralled into character assassination as he had informed her that she should be grateful for his offer of marriage, that she was in danger of becoming an old maid, harnessed to her job, no time for men. Every cancelled date had been paraded in front of her as evidence of her inability to have a successful relationship.

If this was him banging on the door, pleading for a second chance, then she could be brutal too.

Shame she just felt so wrung out and disillusioned. She had returned to her house, feeling soiled, had quickly got out of her clothes and piled them into the washing machine, as if a good clean would rid them of bad memories, and was now wearing faded grey track pants and a baggy teeshirt.

She pulled open the door just as far as it would go with the chain still in place, which was sufficient for her to see that an apologetic Sam was not the man who had been banging on her door. Relief was very quickly replaced by suspicion.

'What are *you* doing here?'

Rocco, unable to come up with a reasonable answer to that, since he didn't know himself, lounged indolently against the doorframe and stared down at her, all dark, brooding male.

'Are you going to let me in? Why do you have a chain on your door, anyway? Dangerous out here, is it? Lots of people you might want to keep out?'

'One or two,' Amy said, meaningfully.

'Well? Are you going to let me in? Or have I caught you in the middle of…something?' His eyes swept over her, took in the change of clothes. 'Unlikely outfit for seduction,' he muttered, 'but who am I to say what turns other people on?' He stuck his hands in his pockets and edged his shoulder just a little bit closer so that she would literally have to bang the door on him if she wanted to shut him out, risking dislocating something in the process.

'I'm not in the middle of anything,' Amy snapped, releasing the chair and yanking open the door so that he could come in. 'And don't be disgusting.'

She turned away and heard him call from behind, 'Sex is never disgusting, even if you approach it in baggy sweats.'

'What are you doing here? No, don't tell me. You've come to fill me in on what was said at the meeting I *should have* attended, but was too frivolous to go to. Do you *ever* stop working?' She had been heading for the kitchen, which seemed the most impersonal space in which to sit down and discuss business, and as she turned around she realised that he was a little closer on her heels than she had thought. In fact, she very nearly bumped into him. And her question about whether he ever stopped working was not exactly one she wished she had posed, because the darkening in his eyes as he looked down at her was giving her a very giddy answer.

'Coffee?' she asked hastily, picking up speed and heading for the kettle with a feeling of deep relief. 'Have a seat at the table and you…you can tell me what was said. Although, I *would* have come to your office in the morning to be filled in.' She busied herself with cups, acutely aware of him sitting there and following her every movement with those amazing eyes of his. He looked slightly dishevelled and all the more unnervingly attractive for it.

'I thought you might have been here with the boyfriend,' Rocco said, stretching out his long legs at an angle and linking his fingers loosely together on his lap.

'So that you could have another go at him, you mean?' At the mention of Sam, she could feel herself tense. She didn't want to talk about him and could never confess what he had said to her, the insults he had dished out that had been too close to the mark for comfort. She didn't want to acknowledge her failure as a woman just yet, not to herself and certainly not to this man sitting here in her kitchen, who had probably never suffered a sense of failure in his life before.

She reminded herself that he wasn't here because of her private life. He had come for a purpose. Business.

'Was I doing that?'

'You know you were,' Amy answered sharply. 'All that pretend interest in what he was saying. Mr Tycoon meets Mr Ordinary and puts on a show of being curious.' She slammed the cup down on the kitchen table and muttered a belated apology.

Rocco's jaw hardened and he thought that perhaps this hadn't been a very good idea at all. Listening to her defend her boyfriend was combining with the after effects of three glasses of whisky rapidly drunk in succession to give him a sickening headache.

'Mind if we take this through to the sitting room?' He turned his back on the half-formed protest and headed straight to the sitting room, where he proceeded to monopolise the long sofa, stretching out on it so that his feet edged off the bottom arm. 'Slight headache,' he informed her before she could launch an abortive attack.

He didn't look dishevelled, she thought restlessly, he looked worse for wear and the headache would explain it. Suddenly, seeing him stretched out like that, nursing a blinding headache, he looked stripped of his arrogance and oddly vulnerable.

'Do you want…something for it? Some aspirin? I've got some in the kitchen…'

'No, it'll pass but no lights, please. Not just at the moment.' Which just left the faint light from the hallway filtering in. The savage turmoil in his head seemed to be easing. Well, he thought dryly, he hadn't really been lying about having a headache. Might not be quite what she thought, but, literally, his head had been aching from an unusual bout of discomforting thoughts and, strangely, here it seemed to be easing.

'I found those cuttings.'

'I beg your pardon?'

Rocco inclined his head so that he was looking at her, liking the way she was leaning forward on the chair, leaning into what he was saying.

'The scrapbook my father kept. I suppose you knew that I'd hunt it down.'

Amy's face cleared and she half smiled. 'A little temptation…is good for the soul. Remember you said that? Do you want to talk about it?' Suddenly discussing her future and the future of her colleagues no longer seemed very important. Right now, she wanted him to discuss himself and just recognising that was like leaning over a very high precipice. One that left her heart beating wildly and made her throat feel dry.

'Why would I want *to talk about it?*' Rocco grated, obeying a lifetime's instinct of guarding his private life.

'No reason.'

'I hadn't expected *quite* so many clippings,' he said grudgingly, propping his arm under his head.

'He took a great deal of interest in what you were doing.'

'There were snapshots there as well,' he informed her. 'I have no idea why I'm telling you this.'

And don't start getting the wrong idea. Amy heard the subtext and wondered whether he was as aware of it as she was. Maybe it was just habit, a long ingrained habit of silence that had become a part of him, like a second skin.

'We can discuss the meeting if you would rather,' she

said helpfully, sipping her coffee and unable to tear her eyes away from his supine form.

'Photos of when I was a kid.' Rocco laughed harshly. 'I can't even remember having them taken. Some were posed, but others…the old man must have been standing there, with his camera, taking the odd shot when I wasn't looking.'

'Parents do that.'

'Not mine. Mine sent me packing as soon as was legally possible. Anything to get rid of the kid who reminded him of his beloved wife who died in childbirth.'

'I'm sorry.' Clear, curious eyes met his without pity or judgement.

'Don't be. It's not your problem.'

Rocco felt as if he were climbing out of his skin. Revelations of a personal nature were things other people did. Soft, self-indulgent people who lacked the strength to tackle their private problems without useless words of comfort from blithering do-gooders.

'Which doesn't explain why he would take pictures of you and keep them…if the only thing he wanted was to get rid of you…'

'Beats me,' Rocco heard himself say gruffly, and Amy gave another one of those little shrugs that made him somehow think that whatever she was saying, it wasn't because she was being nosy.

'Did you ask him?'

'What?'

'Did you ask him about the clippings and the scrapbook?'

'Have you lost your mind?'

'Maybe you should. How else are you ever going to get your answers?'

'He needs rest…besides, he'll be on his way to Italy

soon…' Rocco pointed out. There was a time not very long ago when anyone even daring to pose such a question to him would have been treated to instant dismissal. There was a time, too, a little voice said, when the situation would never have arisen in which such a question could have been posed.

'You could give him time to settle and then you could always fly over and see him face to face.'

The silence that greeted this was telling. In it, she could guess at a wealth of insecurity at confronting the man from whom he had been estranged ever since he had been a child.

She slipped from the chair and went to the sofa, squatting down right in front of him and horribly tempted to reach out and touch him. This semi-darkness was all very well for headaches, she thought with agitation, but it was wreaking havoc with her common sense. Rocco Losi needed her help about as much as a lion needed an ant. And now that she was here, inches away from him, her well-intentioned heart was hammering with a feeling that had nothing to do with comforting him out of his temporary vulnerability.

She began edging a little backwards and was unprepared for his hand reaching out to cup the back of her neck.

'No, stay. I like that. I like you right here.'

Right here, within touching distance, he added to himself. With blinding clarity, he realised why he had come here. Never mind the whisky and the muddled thoughts. He had come here because he had had to make her see just how stupid she was being in accepting that man's offer of marriage. Security was important, but it wasn't worth sacrificing your life for.

He gently stroked the back of her neck and her eyes widened.

'You…wanted to talk about the meeting…' she suggested breathlessly. Those long fingers were doing things to her body, just as his lips had done when he had kissed her that time, except now it seemed different, because this was happening so slowly.

'In time,' Rocco said softly. The hand left the nape of her neck so that it could stroke some hair away from her face and finally settle on her jawline. 'Do you feel sorry for me?' he murmured.

'I will if you want me to. I think perhaps you made a mistake somewhere along the line, and maybe your father did as well. Pride can kill a relationship, but, hey, we all make mistakes.' She lowered her eyes, thinking of the one she had made and the even bigger one she had escaped from, because marriage to Sam would have been all wrong.

Rocco, watching her lowered eyes, sensing the compassion, felt a fierce twist of anger that she couldn't see the huge mistake she was on the point of making herself.

His hand, gently stroking her jawline, pulled her towards him and his lips met hers with an intensity that had been building up for days. He urged open her mouth, wanting to explore every damn inch of her, starting from the top and working his way downwards. It was unprincipled. She was an engaged woman. Good God, she had probably set a date for the wedding! Rocco, who was deeply and fiercely territorial, had never contemplated a married woman, or any woman who was involved with another man, for that matter. But this woman was an exception. He told himself that he was saving her from herself. And whether she knew it or not, she wanted to be saved or else why would she be kissing him the way she was? Her body ripely surging towards him, eager to be touched?

'I need you to lie right here beside me,' he commanded hoarsely.

'Rocco…'

'Shh. Don't talk. You want this. We both do.'

Amy sighed. Every fibre in her body was trembling. This wasn't the sort of man she had ever imagined herself being drawn to, not in her wildest dreams. She had spent her adult life knowing that security was the one thing she needed so badly. Most of her life had been wrapped in insecurity and love, she had always thought, was something safe, something that she could wrap around her like a blanket.

Rocco Losi wasn't secure and he didn't follow the rules of the game as she knew it. He was a predator who saw what he wanted and took it and, once he had it, saw no reason not to discard the possession as soon as he tired of it.

Every shred of self-preservation told her to run away as fast as she could, but when he touched her like this, and whispered in her ear, she felt faint with a craving that was like a monster that had been lurking, unseen, somewhere deep inside her.

She crawled onto the sofa with him and curved into his body, loving the hard length of him pressed against her.

'God, this feels so good,' he murmured. He tilted her head back so that he could kiss the slender column of her neck. Just taking it easy, slowing the pace, was driving him nuts. No perfume. She tasted sweet and fresh. Just as he had known she would. There was nothing artificial about her, no war paint to create an illusion, no scent designed to lure, no conversation that wasn't heartfelt.

'Does this feel good for you too?' he asked, needing to

know the answer and blindly running his hand underneath her jumper until he felt the swell of her breast.

'Too good,' Amy murmured softly back and the little catch in her voice sent his senses spiralling into orbit. He wanted to stroke every small inch of her and erase every touch of every man who had ever touched her. He wanted her thoughts, her mind, her body to be his.

'Undress for me.'

It wasn't a request. It was a demand and it sent a ripple of excitement racing through her body.

Amy struggled up, thankful for the darkness so that he couldn't see her blushing, because stripping off with a man's gaze on her was something she hadn't done before. Least of all, stripping off knowing that she was being watched. She whipped the jumper off, dropping it on the ground, and then reached behind her to unhook the bra strap.

Rocco had propped himself up alongside her, and his hard body was all shadows and angles.

Thank goodness the sofa was as huge as it was, she thought, slowly drawing down the straps of her lacy bra and feeling the aching weight of her breasts as they were released from their confinement. She had bought the sofa with the intention of having something big enough to stretch out on in front of the television, to fall asleep on with room to spare. It could have been designed as a love nest, and just as well because she didn't think her wobbly limbs would go very far to making it up the stairs to her bedroom.

'Lie back.'

'Do you *always* give orders when you're making love…?' Amy asked, basking in his male domination, loving it in fact.

'Any objections?' In the dim light, she saw his mouth

curve into a crooked, amused smile and she shook her head and did as he had ordered, stretching back so that her arms dangled over the back of the arm rest.

Then it was her turn to watch him as he eased himself off the sofa and stood up so that he could remove his clothing.

His body was magnificent. Broad shoulders, tapering to a narrow waist and lean hips, long, muscular legs. He had the sort of pin-up body that women fantasised about. And he was attracted to *her?* After the verbal battering she had endured earlier on, that in itself was a powerful kick to her ego.

She moaned softly, half closing her eyes as he tugged the bottoms of her track pants, teasing her about the novelty for him of stripping a woman of something as unglamorous as what she was wearing. But there was something almost tender in his voice even though she knew that he didn't *do* tenderness.

His naked body, as it joined hers on the sofa, depressing it so that she rolled into him, felt shockingly *right*.

She curled her arms around him and then kissed him with mounting urgency, loving the throb of his manhood against her.

With a thick groan, Rocco pushed her back and then trailed his lips along her collar-bone, edging downwards to breasts that were aching to be touched.

He wanted to feast on her. But first, her breasts, small but perfectly formed with large nipples that were made to be licked. By him. He massaged first one with his hand, rolling his thumb over the hard nub until Amy was writhing against him, until she had to press his head against her so that she could feel his mouth covering what his thumb had been stroking.

A thousand sensations splintered inside her as he suckled her breast, drawing her nipple into his mouth so that he could roll his tongue over the sensitive peak, and when his hand rested against her inner thigh she had no hesitation in doing naturally what her pliant, willing body wanted to do.

It was strange, but for a few seconds she seemed to detach from herself and what she saw was not the efficient woman who spent most of her waking time thinking about her projects, contemplating ways to improve what she did. Nor did she see the slightly shy girl underneath who seemed to have been looking for love for ever. Instead, she saw a wanton, uninhibited creature, tossing on a sofa, her cheeks flushed with pleasure, her eyes openly gazing down at the man ravishing her intimately.

Then her thoughts ceased as his hand found the moistness between her legs and began doing things to her that made paradise seem finally within reach.

CHAPTER SEVEN

IT WAS a dizzy ride.

'You can't…' Amy gasped as his mouth left its leisurely exploration of her tender breasts and travelled implacably downwards.

Rocco looked up at her and gave her a wicked smile. 'Can't…?'

'I've never…been touched…there…'

'Where? You mean…here?' And he ruffled the soft curls between her legs with his breath. 'You mean…like this?'

With devastating expertise, his tongue slid between the folds, finding the bud, and Amy moaned and clutched a handful of his springy dark hair between her fingers, feeling his head moving beneath her hand.

Her musky, erotic aroma filled his nostrils and Rocco was seized with a powerful sense of deep satisfaction that he was doing things to her body that no one had ever done before. He was stripping her of her defences and the thought of that filled him like incense. It was crazy. The art of making love, a game he had enjoyed countless times with women who were well versed in the technique, was as nothing compared to this.

Rocco's and Amy's bodies were slick with perspiration and with the risk of doing the unthinkable, of not being able to hold out, he covered her body with his and thrust deep inside her, moving rhythmically, containing himself with great effort until he knew that her climax was only a shadow of a breath away, and then he allowed himself release, feeling a powerful, soaring sense of completion and fulfilment as he shuddered against her.

The sofa suddenly seemed too small now. It had been fine for the furious, urgent pleasure of making love, but right now he wanted to sprawl out on a bed with this woman, hold her against him in comfort and talk.

It occurred to him that the rarefied atmosphere of the country, after the frenetic pace of life in New York, had somehow scrambled his brains. Post-coital chat wasn't something he went in for.

'Can I suggest that we migrate to the bedroom?' he murmured, kissing the corner of her mouth and liking the way she was looking back at him with drowsy contentment, defences still firmly buried away in a box somewhere.

'The bedroom's upstairs,' Amy offered with a smile. 'And upstairs feels like a million miles away just at the moment.'

'In which case, you're very lucky to have your very own knight in shining armour beside you, ever ready to take up the challenge of carrying his woman a million miles up to a bedroom.' He grinned and before she could object had slid off the sofa and was gathering her up in his arms.

Being carried by him felt far too good to warrant a protest, even a token one at the realisation that their clothes had not been simultaneously gathered up in the sweeping embrace. Amy held on, her body still tingling pleasurably from its onslaught.

'Second door on the right,' she murmured, and when he had pushed open the door and deposited her very gently on the bed she turned towards him and smiled. 'I hope that chivalrous gesture hasn't done your back in.'

'I've lifted far heavier weights than you,' Rocco said

with amusement. She was resting against him, with his arm under her head and her face upturned towards his.

'Would your girlfriends like being told that, I wonder?' She had vaguely wondered about his love life, although, in all honesty, from the clippings she had looked at over the years, it had always seemed a predictably shallow one. Rich, eligible tycoon always appropriately adorned with a beautiful, if vacuous-looking, woman on his arm. And from what she had gleaned, none of them lasted very long.

She had unconsciously made her assumptions over time, but now she was deeply curious to find out why this man who, physically and materially, had everything, had not managed to secure a long-term companion.

'Probably not, but since I wasn't actually talking about my ex-girlfriends, then it doesn't matter. I can't say I've ever carried any women anywhere before. You are a first.' He stroked the satiny smoothness of her shoulder. There was something delicate and wonderfully compact about her body. His tendency to always have gone for tall girls suddenly seemed absurd.

'So…? Fill me in, then.'

'I used to work during the summer holidays with a building firm. Part of the duties was to carry some pretty heavy building material. I guess if my back was going to give way, it would have done it then. I like your house, by the way. How long have you lived in it?'

Amy was finding that the relaxed man lying next to her, the one who had pleasured her and taken her soaring to undreamed-of heights, was nothing like she imagined. Was it the sex?

She had a warm feeling of happiness when she thought about making love to him, followed by a swift sensation of guilt. Sam had been out of her life for a matter of a couple of hours, and here she was behaving as though he had never existed.

What must Rocco think of her? It was a jarring note and she shoved it aside.

'Nearly four years.' His hand was warm and firm against her back and she felt a wicked stirring inside her. 'I had just started looking around for somewhere to buy, just something small and functional, and the minute I walked through the front door I fell in love with it. Ideal location, ideal size.'

'And you were in the ideal business to have it renovated…'

'It wasn't done for free!'

'Relax. I was just teasing. All companies carry perks. I like what's been done. Who thought of the wrought-iron door to separate the conservatory from the rest of the house?'

'I did.'

'Clever girl,' he murmured. Her smooth rear was too appealing to resist and he smoothed his hand over it, pressing her against him so that she was in no doubt as to what proximity was doing to his body.

'I believe I *have* already mentioned that…?' For some reason the thought of developing this promising lead into the work arena was not one she wanted to take up. Not when she was melting all over again.

With a self-assurance she'd never known she possessed when it came to the opposite sex, she let her hands travel over his broad, hard chest, down to his stomach, and continued to watch him as she found his stiff arousal, and she didn't take her eyes off his face when she began to play with him.

'Enjoying yourself, are you?' Rocco asked huskily, and Amy grinned and nodded.

'Immensely.'

'Good.' The complacent satisfaction in his voice made her grin broaden. 'Well, far be it from me to spoil a lady's enjoyment…' And his hand left the innocent stretch of her back, where it had been happily doing very pleasant things along her spine, to find the honeyed moistness waiting.

'No need to stop talking,' he instructed in a thick voice.

'What…what were we talking about?'

'Your clever redesigning of your house.' She was beautifully slippery on his fingers and, despite his glib assurance that conversation could be maintained while they enjoyed one another, he was finding it pretty difficult.

'Oh…yes. Mmm. Right.' She sighed and he kissed her fluttering eyelids.

'Perhaps we should hold the conversation…'

This time their love making was slow and languorous and the generous king-sized bed, a simply handmade box squatting low to the ground, allowed a glorious freedom of movement.

Sufficient movement for Rocco to do what he had wanted to do earlier, namely explore every womanly inch of her body, bit by leisurely bit.

He pinned her hands to her sides while he tasted the sweetness of her breasts, licking the stiffened nipples, enjoying her breathless panting as she was held loose captive by his hands on her wrists.

He trailed his mouth along her sides and felt her giggle and squirm, then along her flat stomach, circling her belly button with his tongue.

This time there was no gasp of surprise when he began to taste her with his tongue, just a pleasurable yielding to enjoyment. He even kissed her toes, which were delicate and, to his surprise because he wouldn't have expected it, painted a pale colour, only just discernible in the mellow rays cast off by the lamp he had switched on on the dressing table. He would mention that to her later, he caught himself thinking, and then shook his head to clear it of the thought.

Then it was his turn.

His body should carry an official health warning, Amy thought to herself, because it was just too damned irresistible to the opposite sex.

His flat, small nipples were made to be licked and the hardness of his torso was designed to fit neatly against the soft contours of a woman's body. As she discovered, when she finally positioned herself above him, leaning forward just enough for her breasts to dangle provocatively in front of him with every small movement she made.

She groaned when, eventually, unable to stand the temptation any longer, he cupped them both with his hands so that he could massage them as she continued to move faster and harder until neither could contain the soaring ecstasy of orgasm.

'Wow,' was all Amy could find to murmur as she lay, spent, on top of him.

Rocco was inclined to agree with the description. He tipped her over to his side and then pushed his thigh between hers so that they were wrapped around one another.

'I take it that's a compliment?' Suddenly, the questions that had been nagging at the back of his mind seemed in immediate need of answering. The image of Sam, which had been obliterated by events, rose up in his head and filled it with the bile of pure, undiluted jealousy.

'We have to talk,' he continued softly.

'I hate it when people say that.'

'Did you sleep with him?'

Amy tried to pull away but she couldn't. He tightened his grip so that there was no chance of creating distance.

'Did you?'

The last thing she wanted to do was talk about Sam. Every instinct in her screamed that he was an episode best left forgotten but she could feel Rocco's stillness. She could also feel a dangerous thread of unease snaking through her, reminding her that the pleasure she had just sampled was of a temporary nature. Of a one-off nature, in fact. Reality had never seemed less welcome.

'No.'

Relief coursed through him with disturbing ferocity. *Not that I'm suggesting that I give a damn one way or another,* he would have liked to have added, but that would have been a blatant lie because, as he was fast discovering, he did very much give a damn what this woman did and with whom.

'You mean you went out with a man for months and never got around to sleeping with him?'

'It's not that unusual.'

'Oh, but it is. Highly unusual. And not only did you go out with him, but you had the idiocy to actually believe you could marry the man?'

There were connecting links here, Amy thought in confusion, and she should be getting them but for some reason she wasn't. Her brain wasn't yet functioning at its normal capacity.

'You slept with me.' Rocco, for possibly the first time in his life, was finding it difficult to locate the right way of saying what he had to say.

'I know I did. Look, do we really have to discuss all of this? Now?'

'You must be able to see now that you and that man are totally unsuited. All wrong.' He felt her try again to draw away from him. After what they had both experienced, surely she had to agree with him?

The connecting links were beginning to fall into place. Rocco, for some reason, thought that she was engaged to Sam! That she had slept with him while still being involved with another man!

'I think it's time you went.'

'Because you don't like where this conversation is leading?' His voice acquired a steely edge through sheer frustration. 'Haven't I just proved to you how ridiculous it is for you to even consider getting hitched to a man when you respond to another man the way you did to me?'

So that was it, Amy thought with a swift rush of humiliation and anger. He had made love to her to prove a point. Why he should choose to do that, she had no idea. Perhaps it was simply a case of being away from his country and feeling a bit bored. Maybe he was just finishing up with the point he had attempted to prove the last time he had kissed her. It hadn't worked, as far as he could see, so he had decided to take things one step further because he was the sort of man who never gave up on a mission. She didn't care about the whys, she just cared about the bit that indicated a lack of emotional involvement on any level.

She cringed at the thought of asking him whether that had been the motivation for his sudden attraction towards her, of hearing the fractional hesitation in his voice before he denied it.

'You can't possibly be attracted to him,' Rocco stated flatly, 'if you haven't even slept with him. Sex might not be the be-all and end-all of a successful relationship, but it sure as hell figures pretty high up on the agenda.'

'I need to use the bathroom.'

For a split second, Rocco was sorely tempted to say

no, but he released her and watched as she exited the bedroom. This had all gone wrong somewhere. Okay, so he had wanted to show her, prove to her, that what she felt for that man was illusory, but his explanation now was pushing her further and further away when all he wanted was to draw her closer and closer to him.

When she reappeared five minutes later she was dressed in another fashion-statement pair of jogging pants and a teeshirt and her face was closed.

'So you think that if a man and a woman don't happen to have sex before marriage, then the marriage is doomed, do you?' She took up position on the piano stool at her dressing table and stared at him coldly, wondering how she had ever fallen for the humour, the wit, the gentleness that had clearly all been in her mind now that she had cottoned on to his agenda.

'Come back to bed.'

Amy ignored him. 'You don't think that relationships are just a little deeper than fifteen minutes in the sack. That kindness and security count for nothing.'

'They count for nothing if there is no passion involved.'

She gave a burst of mirthless laughter. 'And you're speaking from a point of experience, are you? Having never been married? Probably having never had any sort of committed relationship in your life before? Tell me where all the passion has got you.'

Rocco ripped off the covers and stood up, his face thunderous. He strode past her, out of the room, and for one bewildering second Amy wondered whether he was going and why his departure made her feel so sick inside. Then she realised that his clothes were downstairs. In their haste to get to the bedroom, they had left both sets of clothes right there on the ground, just where they had been pitched earlier on.

She spun round and raced along the small corridor, down the stairs, to confront him as he was in the process of putting on his trousers. He hadn't reached the shirt yet and she had to keep her treacherous eyes averted.

'So you're going to go ahead, are you? Even though we've slept together, it's still not enough to make you think twice about what you're planning on doing! Security before all else, after all!'

'What gave you the idea that I was planning on doing anything?'

Rocco stopped and stared at her through narrowed eyes. 'I heard you…'

'You heard me…*what?*' There was small comfort to be had from the fact that she was pressed against the wall because her legs still felt as though they were made of jelly.

'When I surprised you at that disgusting restaurant…you were on the verge of telling him…on the verge of accepting his marriage proposal…'

'I was on the verge of telling him that it was all off. You shouldn't jump to conclusions,' she added sarcastically. 'Even you can get it wrong sometimes.'

Very slowly, Rocco slipped on his shirt and began doing up the buttons. 'You saw sense.'

'So there was no need for you to rush in to prove your point!'

'Explain,' he grated ominously, taking a couple of steps towards her. With a halfway decent following wind, she should, she thought in panic, be able to push herself right through the wall and disappear into thin air.

'You heard me! You wanted to show me that Sam wasn't the man for me so you took me to bed!'

'*I* took *you* to bed? Are you telling me that you were just a passive spectator?' Two more steps towards her.

'I...'

He hadn't denied it. He hadn't told her that she was way off target, all wrong, that he had been overcome with lust for her. He was quibbling over details instead. Did he think that she wouldn't notice?

'Yes...?' he asked silkily, doing up the buttons of his shirt. His hair was still rumpled from bed, at odds with the grim expression on his face.

'Okay! So maybe it was a two-way street...'

'Now we're getting somewhere.'

He smiled slowly and panic clutched her throat because she just *knew*, horribly and despairingly *knew*, that one wrong move from him would have her leaping back into bed with him again. Just one of those dry flashes of humour that lurked underneath the forbidding exterior, and she would be lost. And to be lost would be her downfall. Just thinking about it, in a space of a few seconds, and she could see the unravelling of her life because she would want to give herself totally to him, to a man who made a habit of walking away from women.

He was only a couple of feet away from her now and he stretched out his arms on either side of her, caging her in.

'We could spend hours arguing who did what and why, but let's not beat about the bush, Amy. Let's be at least truthful with one another. We made love and we enjoyed it. We enjoyed each other's bodies.'

'And...what...?'

'And...why stop something that we both enjoy?'

'Is this how you operate, Rocco? See a woman, take her to bed and make love just as long as you keep on enjoying it?'

'I don't *take women to bed*. Believe it or not, it's always worked out as a pretty mutual thing.'

'It hasn't occurred to you, has it…?'

'What?'

'That if you had dubious motives for what happened tonight, then I might as well…'

He carried on looking at her, but his body had gone completely still and he was no longer smiling. This was her moment, and she knew it, her moment to call a halt to the crazy roller-coaster ride her emotions seemed to be enjoying, to get her life back in control.

'I just broke up with a man who had asked me to marry him.' Amy kept her eyes fastened helpfully on the top button of his shirt, suddenly grateful that he was up close and personal and not standing at the opposite side of the room, when she would have been forced to take in his whole, imposing figure. Eliminating the face during this speech was definitely an advantage.

'Breaking up might not be a big deal to you, but it's a big deal to me and Sam didn't take it particularly well.' She risked a quick look to find him staring down at her, his face unreadable. And he still hadn't moved a muscle. He was giving her one hundred per cent of his attention and if it was a ploy to make her acutely nervous, then it was succeeding. She drew in a shaky breath and focused. 'So you see, it hadn't been a particularly good night for me, so when you came along…let's just say that I might have thrown myself wholeheartedly into making love with you, the way any girl might given the particular set of circumstances I was going through…'

'Are you telling me that you went to bed with me *on the rebound?*' If the situation hadn't been so tense, the staggered look on his face might have raised a laugh. As it was, she let her silence give him his answer. His totally incorrect but crucially necessary answer.

'It must have happened to you at some point, Rocco.'

'Not so far as I can remember.' He pushed himself away and this time when he looked at her, it was with withering distaste. It was on the tip of her tongue to yell at him that distaste was certainly nothing he should be feeling, considering his own dubious motives in coming to see her in the first place, but silence was a hundred times more effective than speech, and she didn't know where a speech might take her anyway.

'Right.' He headed out of the sitting room, towards the front door, and, after drawing in a shaky breath, Amy followed slowly, keeping her distance. 'Now we've settled this little misadventure of ours, I'll expect you and your team in my office tomorrow afternoon and, this time, make sure you put in an appearance because if you don't, you're out.'

And therein lies the true nature of the beast, Amy thought once he had gone, leaving without a backward glance. Obey or face the consequences, and she had no doubt that he had meant every word of his threat. The prospect of an unfair dismissal lawsuit wouldn't have phased him in the least.

The logical rush of anger kept everything at bay until she was finally in bed, in the same bed they had shared only an hour before. It still carried the masculine scent of him, and after five minutes she went into the guest bedroom to sleep, resolving to make sure that all the linen in her bedroom was washed the following day.

Then the anger dissipated. All she was left with were memories of their bodies entwined as one. She had never given herself so completely to anyone in her life before and it had felt right. She had disliked him in the beginning, and when she thought about it she still couldn't quite figure out when the change had happened, when she had started to see beyond the one-dimensional figure to the man underneath. She just knew that by the time he'd first touched her, he had no longer been the same person she had railed against in her office what seemed like a million years ago.

And it hurt to know that he had walked away thinking the worst of her, thinking that she had used him as a means of getting over a difficult evening with an ex-boyfriend.

He had been right, of course. Security didn't matter one jot if there was no passion involved and she had been a fool to have ever thought otherwise. She had let her background teach her the wrong lesson. Which, she thought, eyes shut, didn't mean that Rocco Losi, with his passion and expertise in bed, was right.

But she wished he were and she fell asleep wishing it and then woke up seven hours later with the jaded feeling of not having slept at all.

And running late.

She spent the morning looking at her watch in an attempt to organise her time, and by lunchtime had to phone Marcy from her mobile and tell her to go ahead to Head Office without her.

'Not a good idea, Amy,' Marcy said with lavish emphasis. 'Somehow I don't think the boss man will appreciate you not turning up a second time. And we won't either. I mean, have a heart, we still need to find out how your dinner with Sam went...'

'Don't worry, I'll be there...I should be through here at the council house in under an hour and I'll just grab a sandwich to have on the way in my car...'

Which didn't reckon on roadworks heading out, forcing her off the main road and down a honeycomb of streets that ate up twenty minutes of her time, and then yet more traffic as she approached Stratford with a one-way system in operation in the town centre to accommodate an open-air market.

She arrived nearly forty minutes later and swept into the boardroom with barely a knock on the door.

'Sorry. I got held up in traffic.' All five members of her team were sitting in a group at the top of the board-room table, which was long enough to accommodate twenty, and Rocco was lounging against the window sill, ankles crossed, leaving no one in any doubt as to who was in charge.

'And who would like to fill in Miss Hogan on what she's missed?'

So they were back to formal modes of address. Well, she shouldn't be surprised, but there was still a dull ache inside her as she dutifully took a spare seat next to Dee and clasped her hands on the table.

There was an awkward silence, during which Amy began to feel a prickling of unease, and then Rocco was speaking again, his voice cool, controlled and dispassion-ate.

He was telling her, apparently, what he had told the board of directors that very morning, and what he would be telling the remainder of the staff the following morn-ing. That his father had decided to resign from actively running the company, although he would remain in con-trol of the shares. This was based on advice from a series of specialists and on the advice of his family in Italy, who, it transpired, had actively urged him to remain in Italy when he got there, where the weather would be better for him. In the e-mails they had shared, Antonio had men-tioned nothing of any of this, and, although she was numb with shock, she could understand why. Partly, he would have shied away from disappointing her, but profession-ally he would have known that such news would have to be broken by the man flatly imparting it for her information.

'This has left me with a few choices. Option one would be to sell the company as a going concern and recommend the directors for voluntary redundancy. Option two would be to entice two of the board members into positions of part ownership, which my father would accede to. Option three would be for me to take over running of the company full time.'

He pushed himself away from the window sill and moved to the head of the table, planting his hands on it and looking directly at her. 'What would you suggest, Miss Hogan?'

'It wouldn't be my place to suggest anything, Mr Losi, especially when I expect you've already made up your mind anyway.'

He straightened, pulled out the chair at the top of the table and sat down, where he still managed to dominate the gathering even though he was now on their level.

'Correct assumption. I've already made up my mind. I have decided to take over Losi Construction. I intend to buy out my father's shares, thereby making him wealthy enough to do precisely what he wants to do for the rest of his life.'

'And your company in New York?'

'I will sell to the highest bidder. There has been enough pounding at my door for the past five years. If my management over there want to attempt a buyout, I will give them a favourable hearing. With some of the profits from the sale of my interests, I intend to take Losi Construction into the twenty-first century, which will include setting up a major subsidiary in central London. That about covers what we discussed before Miss Hogan arrived, wouldn't you agree, everyone?' There was a low murmur of assent and a lot of fidgeting. Rocco pushed his chair back so that he could cross his legs, ankle resting lightly on his knee. Amy was the first to break the silence, taking the lead with a sinking heart. Crunch time had had to come and here it was now.

'So what happens next? To…to us?' She looked anxiously at the worried faces at the table, a far cry from the boisterous camaraderie they had all enjoyed together before Rocco had appeared on the scene with his dire warnings and threats.

While she had been gallivanting with him, she thought guiltily, wallowing in her new-found sensuality, she had forgotten to fight him. Had that been a deliberate ploy he had used? Distract the inconvenient woman and watch the problem go away? She didn't think so, but then she was realising how opaque he was and how useless she was when it came to reading the male species.

'What happens to you…' Rocco looked at each of them one by one, and then proceeded to point out their unique talents. One by one. He must have read all their CVs because he didn't miss a beat. 'So here's what I suggest and you can take time to mull it over…'

Amy didn't think that he could ever come up with something that would have pleased her team. They had worked for so many years doing something they loved, but he proved her wrong.

The offer to those who wished to relocate to London, where they could be linchpins building up the subsidiary organisation and enjoying all the financial benefits that would entail. They would be given their own departments and Marcy, who had always acted as administrator, would be responsible for donating a percentage of the profits to charitable concerns. In addition, they would be given permission to collude on a certain amount of charitable projects each year, which they could then delegate to a team especially created for the purpose.

Rocco would have his talent where he wanted it, Amy realised, and any labour entailed in charitable projects would be of the brawn and muscle variety. To top it off, he mentioned pay increases that had them whispering excitedly to one another.

For anyone wishing to stay, they could expect pay increases and, although they would have to transfer their work base to the head office in Stratford, they would be highly compensated for any necessary house moves to accommodate the change of working location.

It was a clever plan, particularly considering the fact that the majority of the team were free, single and unengaged and therefore prime candidates for a move to London. Yes, they would continue doing some charitable work, but nothing on the scale they had been doing. The sop for that would be the obligatory donations controlled by Marcy and given with the blessing of the board.

He finished talking, sat back and linked his fingers loosely together on his lap.

'Go away and discuss it,' he advised them, 'and we'll meet again in say…about one week's time. I'll get my secretary to fix it up.' There was an obedient shuffle as they all trooped quietly towards the door, Amy at the back of the procession. She was closing the door when he called her back.

'And shut the door behind you.'

She did, but instead of moving to the table she remained with her back to the door and her hands behind her.

'So you won.'

'I've cut a fair deal.'

'This wasn't what your father intended when he first set up the—'

'But every member of your team will accept my offer. More than that, they'll appreciate it for the generous one that it is.'

Amy could feel her heart pounding inside her. 'So you won.'

'It's not about winning,' he said impatiently. 'What I have done makes sense. Your team will see that because they are not blinded by emotion.'

'I'm not.'

'What you've been doing has been more than a job for you. It's been your salvation, your life raft at a time when you needed one. Grow up, Amy, and face the real world. Climb out of your little hiding places and start realising that there is no such thing as a comfort zone!'

CHAPTER EIGHT

ROCCO studied the letter on his desk. Less than a letter, really, but more than a scribble. Just a note laying out the facts that Amy Hogan, having happily worked for several years in the employ of Losi Construction, had now decided to tender her resignation so that she could pursue other career options. She gave the obligatory thanks to everyone who had helped her along the way and made her stay at the company as enjoyable as it had been.

He reached for the telephone, thought again and then settled back in his chair with a frown.

It had been ten days since he had spoken to her and her team, during which, with the exception of her, they had all unanimously accepted his offer of what he liked to think of as an upgrade in their working situations.

She, on the other hand…

Several conversations, all at his bequest, during which she had sat stony-faced opposite him, politely repeating that she wasn't sure long term what she intended to do. Equally politely, she had gone through bits of paperwork with him, made helpful lists of contacts with whom she had built up relations assiduously over the years and annotated telephone numbers that she seemed to have kept stored intact in her head.

And whenever he had tried to edge the conversation away from business, she had given him a look of such utter blankness that he had swiftly moved back to the matter at hand.

All in all, it had been a frustrating week. Frustrating

because she had lodged in his head like a pernicious little insect, distracting him from the hugely important and pressing work concerns he had to deal with.

And now this.

Rocco looked at the letter again, tempted to pitch it in the bin, knowing that such an impulse would solve nothing.

Nor would he be able to see her in the morning, because he was going to New York to deal with the sale of his own company over there.

Rocco pushed himself away from the desk and began prowling restlessly through the room, pausing to stare frowningly at the various artefacts on the bookshelf and the touches of his father that singled out his surroundings as his own. He picked up a little wooden horse, on which a rider in full armoury was reading an open book, and delicately turned it around in his hands, feeling that same sensation that had struck him over the past few weeks, ever since he had unearthed the scrapbook. A feeling that there was something happening under the surface, the surface that he had dismissed so thoroughly years ago when he had left England, something that needed to be sorted out.

He replaced the artefact but remained where he was, thinking. His phone line buzzed and he glared at it with undiluted irritation.

The situation could not go on. He couldn't have his head filled up with images of some employee who had not even been grateful enough to accept the very generous offer he had extended.

Nor of some employee who...

The sheer enormity of the blow his pride had suffered on being told that he had been little more than a man on the rebound still made his head reel with rage. Rocco, so used to controlling situations, events and people, was literally shaken to his foundations at the mere thought that he had been controlled. He still couldn't believe it. Not really. Cornered, he knew that she would inform him otherwise. Unfortunately, even when they had been sitting next to one another discussing telephone numbers and business contacts, he had been unable to corner her. And he was left with the gut-churning possibility that he had been used.

That, more than anything else, was what propelled him to do the one thing he had resolved not to do throughout the course of the day, when the idea had first inserted itself in his head and then proceeded to take root.

At six-thirty, with everything in order for his flight to the States the following day, he drove to her house.

His head was telling him to let it go. She had handed in her letter of resignation and he could easily release her from any one-month notice. The project she had been working on could be completed by other people.

His emotions, however, had been stirred to a point where cold logic, the invaluable tool that had been at his aid for the past decade or so, was no longer a factor in the equation.

Cutting through the convenient packaging of being philosophical and taking on board that you won a few, you lost a few, a streak of raw anger and a desire for some kind of retribution for having been used by her burnt like bile inside him. The fact that she similarly thought herself to have been used by *him* barely featured in his internal, warring debates. In fact, didn't feature at all.

He arrived at her house at a little after seven-thirty, half expecting to find the place empty even though he knew that an employee who had handed in her notice would certainly not be enamoured at the thought of doing overtime. Dedication to a career could take predictable nose-dives in situations such as that.

Typically, she was home. Her car was parked outside. After several jabs on the buzzer, though, it occurred to him that she must have spotted his car drawing up and had decided to simply ignore his presence altogether.

With yet another unaccustomed burst of uninvited, unwelcome and frankly disorienting emotion, he pounded on the door, quite happy to draw attention from anyone who happened to be passing by and from whatever neighbours were around.

His hand was raised for a repeat bang when the door was pulled open and there she was, standing staring up at him with understandable annoyance.

'What are you doing here?'

'You look bloody awful.'

'Thank you very much but you still haven't answered my question. Why are you here, pounding on my door?' The really crazy thing was that as she saw him there now her heart lifted. Noticeably, treacherously and pathetically. She blew her nose vigorously into her hankie, which she then tucked back into the pocket of her dressing gown.

'We have a little something to discuss…' He waved her resignation letter at her and, taking full advantage of her momentary distraction, pushed himself through the front door and into the hallway.

'Not now, Rocco. I'm…I'm not feeling very well…'

'In which case, you need to sit down as quickly as possible and relax. Just let me lead the conversation.'

Relax? With him under the roof? He must be joking! She would have been more relaxed in a fish tank filled with piranha.

'What's wrong with you?' He scooped her up, ignoring her shocked protests, and swept her into the sitting room,

where he proceeded to lay her on the sofa. 'You're hot.'
He frowned and put the back of one cool hand on her
forehead.

'I have a cold, Rocco. That's all. But I'm sorry. I really
am not up to discussing that letter of resignation.'

'No, of course you're not.' He frowned again. 'And
there's no point in you being in the sitting room. You will
be far better off in your bedroom, in your bed.'

'I'm fine…'

'No, you're not.' He picked her up once again, as easily
as if he were picking up a feather. He seemed to be making quite a habit of toting her around, she thought dazedly,
too weak to fight him off.

'Okay. You win,' Amy said as soon as she was on the
bed, dressing gown still pulled tightly around her. 'I
handed in my resignation because I just don't want to
continue working for Losi Construction with you in
charge. I know you'll probably think that it's a case of
sour grapes because I couldn't persuade you to hang on
to the subsidiary, let us all continue what we've been doing, but it's not. Everyone in the team thinks you've been
hugely generous with them and I'm pleased for all of
them, but what you're offering just wouldn't suit me…'

'Have you seen a doctor?'

'What?' Amy blinked, disconcerted by this abrupt tan-
gent.

'A doctor.'

'Of course I haven't seen a doctor! I have a *cold*!
There's nothing a doctor can do about a virus. I may not
have gone to college or university, but I do happen to
know that viruses just have to clear themselves out of your
system.' She sneezed, as if her body were cooperating in
proving a point, and subsided into the pillows with an
involuntary groan of sheer exhaustion. 'I've said all I have

to say on the matter of my resignation, Rocco, so you're free to leave. And in case you might be thinking that I'll skip off now that I've handed in my notice, I won't. As soon as I'm better, I'll be back there working for my obligatory one month.'

Rocco was only half listening to her as he continued to scrutinise her flushed cheeks and overbright eyes. 'Would you hang on a minute? I have a call to make.'

Amy nodded in complete bewilderment and frustration as he flicked his mobile out and dialled into it, walking out of the room as he did so and gently closing the door behind him.

She wasn't surprised that he had hunted her down to quiz her about her resignation. He had been magnanimous in victory, offering sizeable carrots to everyone in the team in order to lessen the blow of disbanding them. He would have expected her to have reacted with the same grateful alacrity as everyone else had. She had felt his mounting irritation over the past few days when they had been together that she had been unable to commit to accepting his offer. So, naturally, being confronted with behaviour that did not tally up to what he'd expected would have had him winging his way to her front door with all the predictable questions. Just to make sure that she fully understood the deal she was rejecting.

She felt too weak to argue the toss right now and she had no intention of making him think that he was the perfect boss who had come up with the perfect solution to an inconvenient problem. She wasn't going to pander to his need to always be right either by allowing herself to be talked out of her resignation, or else allowing him to think that she was somehow misguided in not taking what was on offer because, as everyone knew, Rocco Losi always knew best.

Rocco Losi, as far as she was concerned, could take a running jump.

She still cringed in shame and horror when she thought of how she had catapulted herself straight into his arms only to discover that he had instigated proceedings merely to prove a point. In fact, she had spent the past week and a half attempting to justify her reaction as perfectly understandable given the circumstances she had been in at the time. She had told him that he had been rebound therapy for her simply to even the score, but the excuse had proved pretty handy when it came to trying to downplay the onslaught of sensation he had aroused in her.

And she reckoned she could just about keep up the charade with herself, if she wasn't faced with him. Looking at him was a cruel reminder that making love had had nothing to do with any rebound feelings. It had just been plain, crazy, uplifting lust of a kind she had never experienced before and had therefore been unable to resist. The sheer force and mastery at Rocco's disposal had required an immunity she hadn't possessed.

But it was easier to face all that in her head if she could cling to some vaguely plausible excuse for her behaviour.

And that, in turn, was easier to do if she didn't have to deal with Rocco face to face.

Which was why she hoped that whatever urgent business call he was engaged in would generate a speedy exit from her house.

She edgily watched the door and then even more edgily watched Rocco as he re-entered the bedroom, this time perching on the bed by her instead of safely standing up by the door, out of harm's way.

'I just spoke to my doctor and, from the symptoms you have, it would seem that you are right about it being a virus of some kind.'

'*You spoke to a doctor about me?*'

'He also happens to be a friend,' Rocco said wryly, 'and I would have got him out here but the trip from New York for a house visit seemed a little excessive.'

'There was no need...'

'You're still my employee, remember?'

'Oh, right. For the time being.' Amy closed her eyes because it felt a lot more comfortable shutting him out of her direct line of vision. And she had to try very hard not to be aware of the fractional touching of their bodies, his thigh a whisper against hers. ''Cause I won't be changing my mind. About leaving, I mean. I've got lots of plans, as a matter of fact.'

'And you can tell me all about them as soon as you've had something to eat.'

Amy's eyelids flickered but she didn't open her eyes. 'You haven't come here to be nice to me.' She yawned and finally looked at him with slumberous eyes. 'And there's no need, even if you *are* temporarily still my employer. In fact, I would feel a lot more comfortable if you left so that I could just get on with the business of being ill without having to make conversation with anyone.'

'I'm going to go downstairs and get us something to eat,' Rocco said by way of response. He had come to throw her resignation back at her and, as an adjunct, to try and manoeuvre the conversation back to that night when they had made love, just so that he could satisfy himself that her wildly, sweetly, sexily responsive behaviour had not been a fiction of his imagination. Having always lived with the arrogant assumption that success with any women he beckoned was more or less a given, Rocco found that the mere thought of her using him to get over her breakup with her ex was a grim blow to his masculine pride.

Now he found that his unspoken plans were ambushed by the sight of her patently miserable in front of him.

'Please,' Amy groaned. 'You don't have to feel trapped into playing the caring employer just because you came here to confront me with my resignation and instead find me bedridden with a cold. I took some paracetemol earlier and they should start kicking in pretty soon. In fact, I think I feel better already.' Rocco, duty-bound to behave like a gentleman, was almost as bad as Rocco, hell-bent on proving a point even if it entailed sleeping with her.

Lying here on the bed, with a day's worth of fever-induced perspiration making her face look shiny, and a bedraggled dressing gown that only just managed to pass muster as an item of clothing, was bad enough. Throw Rocco into the equation and it all became a nightmare. She didn't want his eyes roving over her in all her bare-faced plainness.

But he was determined not to go. Amy wanted to cry in sheer frustration.

'When did you take the tablets?'

'I can't remember. About half an hour ago.'

'I've already been here for over half an hour.'

'Well, then, maybe an hour ago! I didn't check my watch at the time!' She half struggled up to make her point but the effort was too much and she flopped back onto the pillows and sighed elaborately.

She watched through half-closed eyes as he disappeared out of the door and returned a couple of minutes later with a cool, wet wash rag, which he proceeded to position on her forehead.

'That should bring the fever down a bit.'

'You've done this before, have you?' Amy said sarcastically, to cover her own acute state of internal hyperactivity at the gesture, and the question was met with an uninformative grunt.

No, he most definitely had not. Rocco headed down to the kitchen to see what he could rustle up, his thoughts on the girl he had left lying on the bed upstairs. Sickly women and tending them had never been on his fast-moving agenda. In fact, he could distinctly remember a number of dates he had cancelled having been accosted with rasping voices down the end of a telephone line. He was no good when it came to dealing with ill health and he made no effort to disguise the fact. To his credit, the three times he could remember having taken to bed he had done the gentlemanly thing and cancelled himself out of his dates, resisting without much effort the eager pleas to care for him, and waiting for his bugs to blow over with barely concealed impatience.

He told himself firmly and unequivocally that, had he known she would be ill, he would never have jumped into his car and driven over, but that once here he had no choice but to at least make sure she ate something.

The something consisted of an omelette for them both and hefty quantities of toast, which he carried up to the bedroom on a tray, along with two mugs of tea.

'And before you tell me that I shouldn't have, I'll inform you that omelettes are one of the few culinary dishes that I'm any good at.'

Amy was just too weak to feel anything but horribly pleased to be taken care of.

'Thank you. I...well, I do appreciate it.' She sat up so that he could deposit the tray on her lap before retreating to a chair by the window with his own. 'Even if I don't need it.'

'Everybody needs a bit of help sometimes,' Rocco said irritably.

'I never get sick.' The omelette was delicious. Fluffy and seasoned and just right.

'Never?'

'Chicken pox when I was eight. I stayed off school for two weeks and enjoyed every minute of it. Since then, coughs and colds and I let nature take its course. This omelette's delicious, by the way.' She glanced up quickly at him and then glanced away. Sitting there by the window, with his arms on his thighs and his plate balanced on the palm of one hand, he looked just a little too disturbingly real for her liking.

She didn't want him in her house, overwhelming her with his blatant masculinity, but, now that he was here, she decided that the only way to deal with him was to treat him with the polite cordiality of an acquaintance. It wasn't worth dwelling on the little technicality that they had slept together, because that would just bring all her nervous, heightened self-consciousness rushing back at her like a freight train in full throttle.

So she proceeded to chat harmlessly about various selected bits of her past, the ones that couldn't lead to any further uncomfortable exploration. She made sure not to go anywhere near the subject of boyfriends, thereby avoiding the possibility of Rocco quizzing her about Sam, which would open floodgates that were much safer firmly shut.

In fairness, though, Amy could talk about Sam until the cows came home, because his absence from her life had been so surprisingly consequence-free. It was somehow shocking to think that she had managed to have a relationship with someone whose overall effect on her had, in the end, been so transitory and nominal.

When she finally ran out of steam, she placed the tray

to the side of her and looked at Rocco with her head tilted politely at an angle.

'I feel much, much better now.' She did. 'I told you earlier about plans I had for after I leave Losi…'

She was doing it again, Rocco thought with a sharp stab of pure frustration. Building up that polite barrier that was as strong as steel and as high as a mountain and, the faster she built it, the stronger was his urge to crash through.

'Your plans…yes…' He moved across to take her tray, thought twice, placed it on the ground and sat on the bed. She had removed the wash cloth from her forehead and he reached out and lightly felt her skin with the back of his hand. 'Good. Fever's going. You were saying…?'

'I…' Amy cleared her throat. 'Yes…I'm sorry I couldn't take you up on your offer…it was incredibly generous and I can understand why the others jumped at it. It was fair as well…but I think it's time I maybe made a complete change of direction.…'

The dressing gown had sagged slightly at the front and Rocco couldn't help noticing the slither of pale skin leading down to her cleavage.

'Yes…' He shifted slightly on the bed. 'I think I cut a very fair deal…'

'It's really something that occurred to me recently,' Amy explained. She leaned forward, her face fired up by that enthusiasm Rocco had first seen when she had talked to him about the work she did, about the hope she brought to people living on estates that appeared to have been forgotten by the rest of society.

'I'm thinking of going back to school.'

'What?'

Amy laughed self-consciously. He was the first person

she had shared this idea with and it was suddenly very important that he gave it the green light.

'Going back to school. Is it such a crazy idea?'

'Not crazy…no…' Rocco smiled slowly, infected by her animation, forgetting the angry reason that had driven him to confront her. 'How long would you be in the educational system?'

'Well, I reckon that I would have to do some kind of access course to compensate for the fact that I never took my A levels, then a proper university course, but one geared towards teaching…I'd have to check it out…'

'And what would you do about money while all this schooling was going on?'

That put a dampener on her high spirits and Amy's smile faded.

'I hadn't given it much thought, actually.' She leaned back against the headboard and folded her arms. 'I had only just begun to play with the idea.'

Rocco pushed himself off the bed, collected the tray from where he had nearly stepped into it on the ground and proceeded to reload his own crockery onto it.

'I'll take this downstairs. Anything else you want? More tea?'

What she wanted, Amy thought, was for him to actually listen to what she had begun saying, but then why should he? He had come to discuss her resignation, to make sure that she got the message loud and clear that if she didn't take the job he had offered, then it was because she was short-sighted and not because he wasn't the model employer. He'd got that and now he couldn't wait to be off.

'So what do you think?' Amy heard herself ask.

'I'll be back in a couple of minutes.'

'I'm absolutely fine now,' Amy replied irritably. 'My colds never last very long and I can tell that this one is on the way out. Food and tablets. Did the trick. If you could just leave the tray in the kitchen and slam the front door behind you. It self-locks.'

Rocco inclined his head to one side, gave her a brief nod and then left the bedroom, shutting the door quietly behind him.

Amy shot a disgruntled look at the closed door and shuffled herself out of the bed, removing the wretched dressing gown *en route* to the bathroom so that she could wash her face and brush her teeth.

Why did he always do this to her? Make her swing into actually thinking that he was human, and interested in what she had to say? That foolish delusion had landed her in bed with him and she was angry with herself now for feeling disappointed that he had calmly left, admittedly on her instructions, apparently profoundly uninterested in anything she had to say about her plans for the future.

She had washed her face and brushed her teeth and was heading back to the bed for an evening with her book and whatever happened to be on television, even if it was just background noise emanating from the portable set on top of her chest of drawers, when the bedroom door opened.

Rocco caught her in a fleeting snapshot of startled surprise. He also discovered what it was that she had been wearing underneath the voluminous dressing gown. Not much. Some tiny shortie pyjamas with a comic-strip character on the front that should have made her look like a kid, but somehow didn't because the vest top was figure-hugging enough to show off her body. His breath caught in his throat. He forgot all about resignation letters and wounded masculine pride. For a few paralysing seconds, neither of them said anything, then they broke the stretching silence in unison, with Rocco telling her that he had washed the crockery and Amy asking why he hadn't left.

'I did say I would come back up to hear about your plans.'

Amy hovered awkwardly, staring at him, feeling practically naked in her attire but with legs that seemed nailed to one spot, unable to dive for cover.

'I only asked you out of politeness,' Amy said stiffly. 'I thought you might like to know considering I'd turned down your job offer.'

Rocco moved into the bedroom and took up position on the same chair he had occupied to eat his omelette twenty minutes previously, freeing Amy to either head for the bed or for the only other chair in the room, which was a squashy one nicely squared by the window. Her reading chair, perfect for curling up in. She opted for the chair because tucking herself under the duvet would have been just a little too intimate for her liking.

'So you want to go back to school,' Rocco drawled. He thought of her going to university, surrounded by lusty men with testosterone levels that were way too high and on the hunt for someone just like her.

Amy curled up in the chair and tucked her feet under her. 'I think, deep down, I always liked the idea of finishing my education. Now I'm being kick-started into doing it.'

'Oh, really.' He sat back and crossed his legs, giving his mind free rein to imagine what this impossibly naïve, impossibly sexy girl/woman might get up to released, for the first time in her life, into an environment where men were as available to sexual experience as the average dog in heat. It was an unpleasantly savage thought. 'Considering that you've been offered the deal of your life, I wouldn't say that the description *kick-started* quite fits the bill, would you?'

'Well, I wouldn't have done it otherwise…'

'And why should you have? Do you understand how difficult it is to make the transition between working and earning money to returning to college?'

'Yes, of course I understand that! I'm not completely lacking in imagination!'

Rocco overrode her protest with fluid arrogance. In fact, he barely registered it. 'Not to mention the sheer hard slog of getting back into the routine of learning, especially when, as in your case, you abandoned it at the age of sixteen.'

Amy felt two patches of hot colour invade her cheeks. The draining lethargy she had felt all day had disappeared, replaced by a surge of furious energy.

'I did not *abandon* my education! I was *forced to leave* because of circumstances beyond my control! All I want to do now is catch up with everything that I missed!'

Her phraseology brought a thunderous scowl to Rocco's face. His mind flew back through time to his own days at university. Born to achieve, he had never suffered the miserable fate of having to work especially hard. Instead, he had landed squarely on his feet and enjoyed everything university had had to offer, including the girls. He had been as keen to explore the boundaries as they had been. He was snapped out of his reverie by her next question,

'Haven't *you* ever wanted to make up for lost time?'

Rocco, caught off guard by her question, flushed darkly.

'Well?' Amy pressed. 'Haven't you?'

'I can tell you're feeling better. You're attacking me.'

'I'm asking you a simple question. That's not attacking,' she said in an attacking voice. 'Antonio says the family would love to see you in Italy, that perhaps you could be persuaded to take a few days off when he's over there. He wants to build bridges. He's old and he's been given a taste of mortality. I'm not the only one who might feel the need to make up for lost time...'

'We weren't talking about me.'

'We *weren't*, but we are now,' Amy said bluntly. 'Go and see him, Rocco.'

'You will make someone a very good wife,' Rocco grated, uncomfortably aware that somehow she had managed to scupper his argument and pin him against a wall. 'You show all the signs of being a nag.'

For the first time that evening, Amy smiled, even though she knew that smiling was fatal, that feeling this warmth glowing inside her like a radiator that had been switched on was even more fatal.

'So will you go?'

'I will think about it.'

'That's not an answer.'

Rocco stood up and began prowling through the room, casting restless sidelong glances at her. 'I'll go,' he finally muttered, scowling. 'Happy?' When she nodded, he paused to stand in front of her, then leaned down to rest his hands on the springy arms of her chair. 'So can we get back to our original conversation?'

'I already know all the pitfalls.'

'You will be entering as a mature student,' Rocco stated, preferring this line of thought to her jabbing inquisition and to the thought of her being surrounded by lusty boys barely out of their teens. 'You might well find yourself like a fish out of water.'

'No more than when I started working for Losi Construction,' Amy retorted. From a safe distance, her lack of appropriate clothing was all right, but with him leaning over her she was acutely aware of the bare skin on display. 'Anyway,' she continued, pressing back into the chair, 'there are an awful lot of mature students on teaching courses.'

'And what about the money?'

'What money?'

'It costs to support yourself for four odd years of your life with no income coming in apart from the basic teaching grant.'

'If you don't go back to your chair, you're going to end up getting my germs.'

Rocco ignored her. 'How do you intend to do that?'

'I happen to have some money saved,' Amy snapped, 'and then there'll be the redundancy package offered by the company.'

Rocco grunted and took himself off to the window just by her chair so that he could perch on the sill and continue to observe her with narrowed eyes. 'Four years is a hell of a long time to live off a limited amount of money.'

'I'm a very careful person.' She twisted round so that she could look at him. 'Anyway, what I decide to do with my life is none of your business.'

'Theoretically, yes,' Rocco drawled, 'but I find that sleeping with someone does allow them a little more leeway when it comes to opinions…'

This time it was Amy's turn to flush but she managed to keep her eyes steady. 'I don't want to talk about that.'

'Fine.' Rocco pushed himself away from the window and strolled towards the bedroom door. 'But here's a piece of advice. If you do go back to school, try to remember that approximately ninety-nine per cent of the boys you meet, and I emphasise the word *boys*, will be sex mad. Nothing to do with love.'

Amy bristled with fury, but managed to hold it in. This was what it was all about. More lessons in how she should take care of herself. Did he somehow see her as his pet mission? The misguided goody-goody whose poor taste in the opposite sex had spurred him on to save her from a potential mistake? An innocent country bumpkin to whom he had been perhaps marginally attracted through sheer boredom and whose naïvety had been a challenge for him, if only to prove that by making love to her he could rescue her from her infernal, foolish ignorance when it came to Sam?

She smiled sweetly at him. 'Which, interestingly, still leaves one per cent. Oh, and close the door on the way out, would you?'

CHAPTER NINE

AMY looked at her reflection in the mirror and gave herself a stern lecture.

The lecture ran along the lines of making sure to avoid Rocco as much as possible. That uphill ambition was sweetened slightly by a process of calm reasoning that predicted that she could manage to do that if she played her cards right and simply scuttled from group to group depending on whether he was there or not.

No problem, she told herself, leaning forward for a closer scrutiny of her make-up. In her head, she had lathered it on, only missing appearing clown-like by a whisker. In reality, she had applied just a shade of translucent powder, some blusher, a light flirtation with dark brown kohl pencil under her eyes and lip gloss. Her hair shone.

Her dress, however, was more of a problem. The sales assistant had persuaded her into a rather daring shade of jade green in a style that even more daringly clung to every inch of her body like a glove, ending just above her knees. A respectable length that didn't seem that respectable given the design. Her high heels added to the glamour factor. Too late to change into anything else, not that she had anything appropriate for the occasion, Amy hoped that she didn't appear tarty.

Really, this occasion shouldn't have been happening. A fortnight ago, she had suggested to her team that she take them out for a leaving do. A restaurant, perhaps. She had duly gone to clear it with Rocco, to ask whether the company would foot the bill, only to run into a barrage of objections culminating in his decision, cunningly veiled as a suggestion, that instead of an isolated small leaving party for just her team they have something rather more elaborate involving all the employees of the company. A sort of thank-you for the effort they had all put in over the years and a welcome to the new start.

'But I wanted something a little more intimate,' Amy had muttered, hovering in front of his desk and evading those brilliant eyes focused on her.

'Your work has involved more than just the members of your team.' Rocco had sprawled back in his leather chair and surveyed her coolly. 'Hardly fair to go for the intimate option and sideline everyone else.'

It had seemed easier to agree. Only a week previously, in fact, precisely five days after he had left her house with her trilling reminder to him that she would be able to manage going back into education and would be looking forward to the mysterious one per cent of men who might not be decades younger than her and intent on climbing into her bed, her team had shifted out of their premises and into the head office. Re-absorption had commenced in earnest. Rocco, having made his mind up, was not hanging about. And he had been in a foul mood every time she had bumped into him in the graceful old building.

In fact, he had been in a foul mood on each and every occasion that he had summoned her into his office to ask for information he had felt he needed from her.

Recently, Amy had taken to ducking into the Ladies whenever she spotted him approaching down the corridor from his office to the partitioned section in which she and her team had been temporarily located.

She hadn't wanted a prolonged argument with him on

the merits and drawbacks of an intimate restaurant for her and her team versus a room booked in one of the top country houses close to Stratford for the entire company. So she had hurriedly agreed, no argument, not even a debate.

Now she realised she was dreading it. At six-thirty, with her silky fringe shawl lightly wrapped over her shoulders, she stepped into the taxi that she had pre-booked and gazed absent-mindedly out of the window as it rushed her along to the venue.

It was hard to believe that she only had a little over one week left at Losi Construction. She had received a lovely, encouraging phone call from Antonio when she had written to him with her plans, had received encouragement from everyone, in fact, but, instead of feeling excited at the Brave New World awaiting her, she felt sickeningly hollow.

And she knew why.

She had had a good few days to come to grips with exactly why she was feeling the way she was, and the only thing that surprised her was that it had taken so long to reach the obvious conclusions.

Not content with fraternising with the enemy, as Sam had once called it, she had fallen in love with him. Oh, yes, she had managed to give herself a load of reasons as to why her heart went into overdrive whenever he was around and why her whole body seemed to come alive simply at the thought of him. She had put it down to the misguided notion that anyone whose plans had the potential to alter the course of her life *would* have had that sort of effect. She had excused her attraction to him on the grounds that his dynamism and powerful good looks made it a simple case of sexual lust, but that she could handle it because she didn't like him. Not really.

It seemed pathetic now that she had admitted the awful truth to herself. She was head over heels in love, in lust, in *everything* with a man who played with women, who had avoided commitment into his thirties as most people would avoid the plague. She had made the ultimate foolish mistake and that was why there was no reason she could even consider working alongside him on a never-never basis. That way lay madness.

She arrived at the country house with her thoughts still free-wheeling in her head and took several deep breaths just standing there, gazing up blankly at the sumptuous stone building with its dominating, coldly impressive edifice, portals guarded by four stately columns. Having visited this particular stately house several times, she was still struck by its perfect English beauty. It lay perched on the brow of a hill, gazing down at some four hundred acres of parkland. Last time she had been greeted by peacocks, which were left free to roam the gardens, but this time there was no sign of them, which was good because they unnerved her.

By the time she had mounted the curving stone steps up to the entrance, her heart was thumping like a trapped bird in a cage.

In fact, thumping so hard that she barely noticed the magnificent surroundings. She just followed the instructions of the middle-aged chap who had been waiting to greet her, took a glass of champagne from one of the girls holding out a tray because she needed something to do with her hands, and walked into a room blessedly packed with everyone from the office.

As with most affairs of this nature, a certain amount of initial effort was made between members of staff who rarely communicated. Amy could see Freddy with a glass of champagne in one hand trapped in a polite conversation with Richard Newton and his wife, Pamela. Several of the younger people, secretaries and their other halves, had already formed their natural groups and were in animated discussion about something or other. In between the eighty-odd people, various waiters and waitresses were circulating with trays of appetisers and drinks. The noise levels were high but she still jumped when a finger lightly tapped her on the shoulder and she swung round to discover that it was only Dee, wearing a dress as white as her hair and looking so unlike her normal self that Amy grinned and relaxed.

'Well, I don't often get to have drinks and dinner in a place like this—' Dee read her expression and grinned back '—so I thought I'd go the whole hog. I mean, you know what my usual garb is, but then again fancy clothes aren't exactly a good idea to wear to work, given where our little place is located. Or should I say *was*.'

'I hadn't intended this when I asked His Highness whether I could cover a meal for the six of us on company expenses.' Amy grimaced, giving one hundred per cent of her attention to Dee and thereby not risking the temptation to glance around her for the man she was trying to avoid.

'*His Highness?*' Dee laughed and shot her a knowing look. 'That's a touch sarcastic considering you two act as though you've got something going.'

'Something going?'

'Not necessarily of a sexual nature, you understand, but there's a bit of electricity there. We've all noticed it, especially this past week or so.'

Amy forced a laugh. 'It's not my fault he's in a foul mood. The man is a law unto himself.'

'Why did you decide to leave?' Dee asked curiously. 'He offered us all a brilliant deal.'

'Like I said, I always wanted—'

'I know *all that*, but why…really…?'

While Amy was struggling to think up a suitably lame answer they were interrupted by a splinter group of the young set and the moment, and the embarrassment of it, was lost.

It still took two glasses of champagne before Amy felt relaxed enough to look around her, interested to see familiar faces and their partners, who were never quite how she imagined them to be. Marcy, Andy and Tim had all brought theirs, and she fell into natural conversation with them, discussing their respective moves and glossing over what she intended to do with herself.

She still hadn't spotted Rocco, but then she hadn't been looking, had been making sure not to look, and by the time she did finally see him they were all on their way into the grand dining room where name cards had been placed on every table. Blessedly she was not on Rocco's. In fact, she was at the table furthest from him, but not so far that she couldn't see just how devastatingly handsome he looked. He dominated the head table, not simply because he was taller than everyone else on it, but because there was something so compelling about the way he stood, one hand in his trouser pocket so that his black jacket flipped over his wrist. Across the crowds, his fabulous eyes were watchful, carefully skimming the assembled groups and disastrously catching hers before she had sufficient time to glance away. The individual voices around her faded into background noise, just a dull throb, and for a few seconds she couldn't breathe. Literally. Then his eyes were moving on, having revealed nothing in their depths when he had looked at her.

Amy couldn't concentrate on the conversation swirling around her. She toyed with her starter, nervously aware of his presence now that she had located the table at which he was sitting. If she hadn't known where he was, she could merrily have continued to focus on what was immediately happening around her. As it was, she found her eyes skittering across the room to find him and hating herself for her weakness when it was apparent from what she saw that *his* eyes certainly weren't drawn to her.

She was barely aware of the wine she was drinking or of the food being taken away and replaced efficiently by yet more food, followed by dessert, which sat on a plate in front of her in an unidentifiable lump, something else to be played with.

The sharp clink of a spoon being tapped against a glass brought her out of her daze as a cup was being deposited in front of her and she realised that Rocco had stood up.

There was no need for him to draw attention to himself again. If ever there was a man born to be a leader and to command attention, then it was him. The noise levels in the room, which had been considerably heightened with the steady consumption of alcohol over the course of the evening, died away, and Rocco remained standing, waiting until there was a hushed silence.

He looked casually, impossibly and unfairly elegant and he moved into speech without the usual clearing of throat or apologetic joke to grab everyone's attention.

Glancing around her, Amy wryly thought that he could have been a hypnotist, because everyone at her table had a mesmerised look on their faces as they listened. She was sure that if he had suddenly pointed across the room to Carl and instructed him to hop like a rabbit, then the apprentice surveyor would have obliged.

He didn't, naturally. Instead, in his deep, sexy voice he thanked them all for their invaluable help while he had been there and their boundless support in the face of necessary changes that had to be made. He cracked a couple of wry jokes before the speech had time to become too heavy, mentioned a couple of people by name, which made Amy realise just how sharp his brain was because even when he had had no idea that he might have been staying on, he had still filed away information that he could pull out of his hat like a magician, had still paid minute attention to the people working with him, had still remembered names from the lowliest member of staff to the most influential.

He ended by raising a toast to his father, much to Amy's surprise, for his foundation of a company that had weathered all manner of setbacks over the years. Then, in the middle of draining the wine from her glass, she heard her name being mentioned and suddenly heads were swivelling in her direction as, embarrassed, she realised that Rocco was now looking at her, thanking her personally for her contributions over the years, informing the assembled crowd that she would be the only member of staff leaving and she would be sorely missed, he was certain, by everyone in the company.

Amy blushed furiously and smiled in a self-effacing fashion at her friends around her.

'And as a show of appreciation...'

Oh, no, she thought, knowing what was about to happen and already dreading every minute of it, please tell me, God, that I don't have to go up there and accept a leaving gift...

'Perhaps Miss Hogan would like to come up and accept a leaving gift from all of us...'

The rousing clapping and cheering had her looking longingly at the exit, then she was being pushed to her feet and propelled in the direction of Rocco, who had now been joined by Marcy carrying a huge gift and by Claire behind her with a bouquet of flowers.

She knew that he was watching her, knew that it would be a massive mistake to catch his eye because if she did she was absolutely certain that her legs would immediately stop functioning and she would topple over and fall flat on her face.

The wine, which had had no effect on her throughout the course of the evening, now seemed to catch up with her bloodstream with a vengeance.

'You're beginning to look worse for wear,' Rocco murmured into her ear as she sidled past him towards Marcy, and Amy tilted her chin giddily but defensively up, ignoring his softly spoken remark.

The thrill of what she had received made her temporarily forget his presence just behind her.

It was an impressively framed collage of all the projects she had ever worked on, starting with her very first, and the broad mounting was signed by every member of the company.

She heard herself stammer out thanks, feeling like an unexpected winner at the Oscars. Her voice was wobbly, which earned her warm applause, and before she could break down completely Rocco took charge and informed the guests that the speeches were over. It was time to have fun and start the dancing. At which point, on cue, lights were dimmed and a DJ, whom she hadn't even noticed, went into action.

'I don't suppose you want to be lugging this great thing around with you for the remainder of the evening...'

Amy stiffened at the expression on Rocco's face. An evening of alcohol and jollity had obviously done very little for his disposition because he was unsmiling.

'I was about to take it outside, get the chap there to keep an eye on it for me. Thank you very much, by the way, for organising it.' Her voice matched his expression although her heart was pounding furiously. Her senses were on full alert, all trace of light-headedness gone, just as all trace of illness had vanished when he had walked through the door of her house almost two weeks previously.

'I'll do it,' was all he said and he lifted the enormous picture and began walking towards the exit.

Amy looked round her to see that everyone was having a great time, throwing themselves across the floor loosely in tune to the music or else in groups, drinking and chatting.

Then she looked towards Rocco's back as he strode towards the exit with her picture and caught between hunting out familiar faces in the semi-darkness or following Rocco, she chose the latter option. Even carrying the heavy, cumbersome object, she still had to walk quickly to catch up with him, which she did just as he was depositing the picture with the security guard and giving instructions that it was to be looked after.

Out of the normal working environment in which she could pigeon-hole him into the category of her employer, Amy felt suddenly conscious of herself, her appearance and her body, so lovingly outlined in its wretched garment.

'Thanks...' She laughed nervously while he perched against the large desk that had been vacated by the security guard who was taking the picture somewhere safe. Half sitting, she was now more on an eye level with him. 'It's a wonderful leaving present.' There was no helpful contribution from him to ease the awkward conversation along. He simply folded his arms and stared at her until she felt her skin begin to prickle.

'Shall we...shall we go back inside? I guess people might start wondering where we are...'

'So how does it feel?'

For one panic-stricken second she had the disorienting feeling that he was reading her mind, that somehow he had clocked what she felt for him and was asking her to explain herself.

'How does what feel?' Amy said faintly.

'To only have a few days to go before you leave the company.'

'Oh. Right. Weird, I guess. It feels weird.' Relief made her suddenly garrulous. 'I've been there for so long that it's become a sort of second home for me, but it's exciting as well, you know…to be facing another challenge…'

'You've been avoiding me. Why?'

'I don't know what you're talking about…'

A few stragglers emerged out into the wide, open hall but were too merry to give them much of a second glance.

'I really think we ought to go back in…'

'Not until this conversation is finished. Come on.' He pushed himself away from the desk and, before her brain could connect, Amy found herself being ushered outside, down the curving stone steps and out into the open lawns.

'Look, Rocco, I'll finish the conversation, but can we go back in?' Darkness and stars in the sky would be just a little bit too much. 'I'm cold.'

'Take this.' He shrugged out of his jacket and slung it over her shoulders and for just the shadow of a second she gave in to the temptation to close her eyes and breathe deeply, breathing in that faint, unmistakable aroma of *him*.

They found a bench and sat down. From here, she couldn't even hear the sound of the music inside and the glory of the manicured lawns stretched around them like a still, dark lake.

'You've been acting like a cat on a hot tin roof every time I've been around and I want to know why.'

'I'm sorry. I hadn't realised…'

'Don't lie to me!'

He had turned to look at her, and his arm was outstretched along the back of the bench.

'It's been awkward for me, all right? Being around you…'

'Why?' Rocco asked softly.

'Employees always feel awkward around their bosses once they've handed in their notice and I know you don't approve of what I'm doing.'

'I don't disapprove of what you're doing,' Rocco said with an edge to his voice. 'I felt obliged to point out the pitfalls.'

'Because you think you can run other people's lives for them?' She turned to face him, but in the darkness it was all shadows and angles and dangerously familiar. 'Besides, you've been in a foul mood lately and it's just easier avoiding someone when they're in a foul mood.'

Rocco shifted uncomfortably on the bench and scowled at her averted face. Yes, he had been in a foul mood. Yes, he had convinced himself that it was a bloody good thing the woman was leaving the company because even when she wasn't physically within eye-range, she was still an unnecessary distraction. In fact, she had been an unnecessary distraction from day one and distractions and work didn't mix.

'I happen to have a lot on my plate at the moment,' he grated. 'Commuting between London and New York doesn't qualify as one of life's more relaxing experiences.'

'Which doesn't mean that you have to take it out on other people.' Amy shrugged and continued staring straight ahead.

'I haven't heard anyone else complaining.'

'That's because everyone's scared of you.' This time she looked at him, shivering as the full force of his proximity wrapped around her.

'Except you…' She looked like a kid sitting there with his jacket over her, a kid who'd rummaged in an adult's cupboard and decided to try on something five sizes too big. No kid, though, he reminded himself, and certainly not the gullible innocent he had felt duty-bound to save from her own destiny. She had kicked him straight in the groin when she had delivered that scathing remark about using him as temporary therapy to tide her over after her breakup. His mouth tightened, yet again, at the thought of it, but he still found himself savagely rejecting the advice from his head telling him to leave the situation alone and to go back to the safety of inside.

'Look at me when I'm talking to you,' he rasped out.

'Or else what?'

Rocco demonstrated by reaching up to curve his hand beneath her chin and a flood of heat licked through her. She looked at him, every nerve in her body alive and alert.

'That's better.'

'You are the most arrogant man I have ever come into contact with, do you know that?'

'But I still make you tremble…'

'I'm going inside. I don't want to have this conversation with you…'

'No, you are not!' His hand snapped out, circling her wrist, and he pulled her back down and now she was sitting so close to him that her thigh was touching his. 'Were you hurt?' he demanded, loathing his weakness in dragging this conversation out when he knew that he was just lining himself up for another gunshot wound to his male pride.

'Hurt by what?'

'Hurt that I've been in such a bad temper towards you…' Her softly indrawn breath and that fractional pause sent a flare of pleasurable certainty rushing through him. He sensed her looking for a way of denying his accusation. He wasn't going to let her have her way and he tossed aside any notion that his reaction was based on avenging his hurt pride. He wanted her back in his bed.

'I just didn't understand…'

'Have you missed me?' He cupped her face with his hand and felt her tremulous response, which gave him a kick of pure satisfaction.

'Should I have?'

'You've missed me.'

Amy was thrown into a state of hideous confusion by the swiftness of his assumptions and their accuracy. In that brief, panicked pause he had leapt to the correct conclusions. Rattled, she now didn't know how to extract herself from the situation and his eyes were pinning her to the bench, making her squirm under their intensity.

'I…I…' she stammered in desperate retreat.

'I've missed you too,' he breathed, startling himself and her with the unexpected confession.

'You haven't missed *me*, Rocco. You've missed being in control because I broke things off, because…'

'Stop arguing.' He leant forward and was suddenly, overwhelmingly aware of how long he had been itching to do this, to lose himself in her lips.

There was no room for protest as his mouth descended on hers and with a soft groan Amy parted her lips so that their tongues met, so that they could explore each other. He grasped the lapels of his jacket, which she was wearing, and pulled her into him, forcing her head back as the kiss deepened and became infused with urgency.

Amy struggled free, intending to push him away, intending to cling to her hard-gained resolutions to walk away from a dangerous involvement, and heard herself mutter shakily, 'We can't…everyone's inside…they'll start wondering where we are…'

Rocco heard the capitulation in her words and a soaring sense of pleasure and satisfaction flooded through him.

'I doubt that very much but if you like we can go inside and say our goodbyes…'

Amy emitted a little squeak of horror. 'No!'

'Then we'll just have to sneak off.'

'Sneak off?'

'Like a couple of teenagers playing truant.'

Before her brain could get into gear, he had stood up and taken her hand, pulling her along to the car park and then depositing her inside his car.

'Wait here,' he ordered, 'I'm going to go and retrieve the leaving presents.'

'We can't. What if…?'

'Life's too short for *what ifs*.'

Amy had fifteen minutes to ponder this nugget of wisdom and then his dark shape was heading towards her, picture in his arms and the bouquet of flowers dangling from his fingers. He opened the boot of the car, dumped both inside and then got into the driver's seat.

Instead of turning on the engine, though, he swivelled around to look at her.

'Are you sure about this?' he asked in a low voice. 'Because if you aren't, this is the time to say so.'

'No,' Amy said truthfully, 'I'm not sure…'

Rocco turned away and she placed one small hand on his wrist.

'I'm not sure because I don't want to end up being hurt and I know that getting hurt is going to be part of the deal, but you're right. Life's too short to worry about the consequences.'

Life was too short, she thought sadly to herself, to think about the empty months stretching ahead once he had walked out of her life, wondering what might have happened if she had thrown caution to the winds and slept with him again.

'Why do you assume that you'll end up being hurt?'

'Because that's the kind of guy that you are, Rocco. You hurt women.'

The whispered assertion was like a stab in the gut, but he wasn't going to deny the truth of it.

'So shall I start the engine or not…?'

'Start the engine.'

She didn't know where they were going, but she wasn't surprised, after twenty minutes during which nothing was said, to find them pulling up in front of the house that she had visited many times before when Antonio had been living there.

She followed him out of the car, waited until he had unlocked the front door and stepped behind him into the dark hall, instantly thrown into light at the flick of a switch.

'I'm going to make you a coffee,' Rocco said, turning to her, wanting her so badly that it hurt and knowing that the last thing he should do was head up to the bedroom. She would come. He knew that. They would make love, passionate, fulfilling love. But without frills, the very act would become nothing more for her than a base exchange of bodily fluids. He had never thought about sex in those terms before but he thought it now and found it distasteful.

Amy nodded and, for the sake of making conversation, asked him about his father.

'I spoke to him,' Rocco said, without turning around. 'It went beyond the polite exchanges we have become accustomed to. Sit down. I won't bother to tell you to make yourself at home; I should think you already know this place like the back of your hand.'

Downstairs, at any rate, Amy thought, with another excited, nervous pang at the thought of what awaited her upstairs.

'I telephoned him two days ago to talk about the company and to ask his advice on certain things. I also mentioned that scrapbook…'

'You did?' Amy smiled warmly just as he turned around to face her.

'I did,' Rocco said dryly. 'I think we are beginning to make headway on the personal problems that have dogged us over the years.'

'You are?' Her smile broadened with delight and Rocco looked at her with amusement.

'You'll make a brilliant teacher…'

Once, she would have been thrown off course by the abrupt change in conversation. Now, she just fell in with the flow, relaxing for the first time that evening and enjoying the easy contentment that filled her when he was like this, at his most charming and open and relaxed.

'Even though I shall be ancient compared to everyone else and won't have enough money to live on?'

'Yes, I'm afraid you will be ancient in comparison…' Rocco smiled at the thought of that '…and as for the money…well, I would never let you go without…'

'Sorry?'

Where the hell had that come from? he thought in confusion.

'Obviously, I would do what my father would have

done, make sure that you were looked after and financially supported wherever possible.'

'Did anyone see you as you were leaving?' If he could change the subject as and when he wanted, depending on whether he wanted to avoid a conversation or not, then so could she, and right now she wanted to avoid any conversation in which he had a starring role as her guardian angel.

'Lots of people,' Rocco answered with a straight face. He sat down at the kitchen table, facing her, and dragged a chair towards him, which he proceeded to use as a footstool. 'I told them that I was bringing you back to my house so that we could make love.'

'You didn't!'

'No, I didn't. Only a couple of people were around in the outer hall and they were too busy babbling over one another to notice me, so I crept out like a thief into the night carrying your picture and the flowers.'

It made an unbearably romantic picture. Rocco had all the physical similarities to make a very convincing cat burglar. Jittery, excited nervousness made her feel suddenly faint as she contemplated the bedroom upstairs, waiting. Now that she had made her mind up, there was no going back. She was in it now for better or for worse. Actually, for worse, Amy thought realistically. Forget about the better bit. She pushed her mug away from her, cupped her chin in her hand and looked him squarely in the face.

'Well? Shall we go upstairs now?'

CHAPTER TEN

SO WHAT, Rocco thought, was with the sudden reluctance? As a fully paid-up member of the red-blooded male club, he should have been taking the stairs two at a time in his haste to get Amy into bed. Hadn't he been the one to make the suggestion in the first place? She had been on his mind, night and day, ambushing him when he was trying to work, feeding his restlessness when he had a thousand and one things to think about of more pressing importance. He had come to the conclusion that sleeping with her would get rid once and for all of the impact she was silently having on him.

And here she was, fixing him with those huge nervous, serious, crazily enticing brown eyes, inviting him to bed. Two and two should make four in an ideal world, but suddenly he was disconcertingly reluctant.

'What's the rush?' he asked, when she stood up and extended one slim hand towards him. 'Don't all members of the animal kingdom perform a courtship routine before mating?'

'I thought we'd already done that with the coffee,' Amy quipped, uncomfortable now. Should she sit back down? He hadn't moved, after all. It occurred to her, just a quick, nagging thought, that perhaps he had gone off the idea altogether now that he had proved that he could have her. Whenever he wanted, and on his terms.

'What a thoroughly modern miss,' Rocco drawled, with an edge to his voice. He was accustomed to knowing precisely where he was going and what he was doing; the confusion he was feeling now, instead of engendering self-analysis, ignited frustrated anger. Anger at himself, anger at her, anger at not knowing why things were suddenly not as straightforward as they should have been. He should have been tearing her clothes off, for God's sake! Instead of sitting here like a wimp!

'One cup of coffee. Is that all it took for your ex-boyfriend to get you into bed?'

A rush of colour turned her cheeks to scarlet and she collapsed back into the kitchen chair.

'What's this all about, Rocco?'

'I asked you a question!'

'And I'm not answering it! I knew...I just *knew* that it was a mistake coming here in the first place.'

'Don't accuse me of arm-twisting,' he grated. 'If I recall, I asked you in no uncertain terms whether you were sure you wanted to!'

'I didn't think...*what's the matter with you?*'

Rocco had no idea. He just felt as though he were uncomfortable in his own skin, and the nasty little incident when she had informed him that he had been nothing more than sex on the rebound, which he had thought he had put to bed, now came rushing back at him with renewed force. He saw the bewilderment on her face and it stoked his anger.

'What's the matter with *me?*' He stood up and began walking through the kitchen, circling the central isle like an untamed predator caught in a trap. He needed to release some of this killing energy. And he didn't want to see her face. He didn't understand what the hell was the matter with him, and incomprehension was fuelling his brooding, angry helplessness.

'I'm calling a taxi.' Amy extracted the mobile phone from her bag with trembling hands and shakily dialled through to the taxi company she always used. She kept one eye on him as she made the call, wondering how she was going to get through the time it would take for them to arrive. She didn't even think that he had realised that she had called a taxi.

'How dare you ask what's the matter with *me?* The first time you slept with me because you needed a bit of sexual therapy and here you are now, ready to sleep with me again without even bothering with the frills of wooing!'

Amy's head snapped round in shocked, hurt rage. Trust him, in his arrogance, to overlook his own behaviour. Did he think that she was some kind of sexual predator? It was such a ludicrous thought that, under any other circumstances, she might have burst out laughing.

'There's no point the two of us shouting at one another,' she said stiffly, her body rigid with tension. 'I got the wrong message. I thought this attraction thing was…was mutual. Now I realise that the only reason you brought me back here is because you still want to avenge your hurt pride!'

'Maybe you're right.'

No, she wasn't going to cry. No, she wasn't even going to allow her lip to wobble. She was going to survive this agony and walk out of this house a better, stronger person. This was going to be a valuable lesson to her in never getting emotionally out of her depth. When it came to matters of the heart, she just wasn't a strong enough swimmer.

Rocco paused with his hip against the counter and frowned across at her, raking his long fingers through his hair.

'Could you blame me?' he growled because her silence was beginning to infuriate him.

Amy shrugged and eyed him warily as he took a couple of steps towards her.

'What does…' he gave an eloquent version of her shrug '…mean?'

He pulled up a chair so that he was sitting facing her, leaning towards her with his elbows resting on his splayed knees. All that was missing was a bright spotlight, she thought, drawing back, and he would be in full interrogation mode.

'I can't believe we came here…you pretended…you just brought me here so that you could accuse me of…stuff.'

Rocco flushed darkly.

'I suppose next you'll be launching into a sermon on how stupid I am to be thinking about changing my career, even though a minute ago you told me that I might make a good teacher.' She could feel her eyes begin to well up in self-pity and bitter disappointment and she lowered them hurriedly.

'I apologise…'

'What for?' Amy looked up at him, eyes flashing. 'You're just being honest, after all. I made a stupid remark and you're making me pay for it!' Their eyes met and it took enormous effort not to be the first to look away. 'But you needn't worry! I've ordered a taxi. It should be here any minute and once I leave this house I'll be out of your life for good! I won't bother coming in to work next week. I've handed over everything already, anyway, and my team are fully capable of taking over in my absence!'

On cue, there was a sharp ring on the doorbell and Rocco pushed his chair back, sending it flying behind him where it clattered into the side of the counter.

Amy grabbed her handbag and raced behind him to catch him aggressively ordering the taxi driver to leave immediately. He pulled out his wallet and she grabbed his wrist fiercely.

'What do you think you're doing?'

'Are you the lady who ordered the taxi?' The cab driver was obviously having second thoughts about the wisdom of coming out for this particular fare.

'I'm paying the man for wasting his time in coming here,' Rocco glowered, shoving a wad of notes to the taxi driver without bothering to count them.

'Yes, I'm Miss Hogan.'

One arm of steel reached across, barring her exit.

'You coming or not, lady?' Having been paid excessively and with the prospect of not actually having to drop anyone anywhere for the money, the taxi driver already had departure written all over his face.

'The lady won't be coming,' Rocco snarled.

'Sorry,' Amy apologised through gritted teeth.

She waited until the front door had slammed and then swung round to face Rocco, hands on hips.

'Thank you *very much*. And how long do you intend on keeping me prisoner here?'

He didn't like that but Amy no longer cared. She looked back on the girl who had excitedly come to the house as someone else, a gullible creature whose heart had been broken but who had made no effort to protect herself from further hurt.

'I think we should have a drink,' was all he said.

He stalked into the kitchen and while she hovered in impotent fury by the door, arms belligerently folded, he poured himself a glass of wine. When he offered her one, she shook her head, barely trusting herself to speak.

Mimicking one of her shrugs, he brushed past her towards the sitting room, expecting her to follow him. Which she did.

'You had no right to cancel my taxi,' Amy began in her best restrained voice.

'We hadn't finished talking.'

'*I* had!'

'Sit down. You look as though you're about to turn tail and run, standing there by the door.'

'I would if there was anywhere to run *to!*' She sighed in annoyance but sat on one of the chairs, waiting for him to talk. He claimed he wanted to talk, then she would just sit and let him fire away.

While she was as tense as a tightly coiled spring, he sprawled back on the sofa, holding his wineglass lightly on his chest, staring up at the ceiling.

'I didn't bring you out here so that I could vent my anger on you,' Rocco said, out of the blue. His fabulous eyes flickered in her direction. 'When we left that party, I was all in favour of a long night of undiluted passion.'

'Then what happened?' Amy whispered, straining forward to hear him. He hadn't bothered to switch the lights on, so that the only lighting was what filtered through the open door leading out into the large stone-flagged hall.

'Then...good question...' He stood up, with his unfinished glass in one hand although he had stopped drinking. She thought that he might actually have forgotten he had it at all. He shoved his hand in his pocket and began prowling through the room, finally pausing in front of the fireplace so that he could rest the glass on the mantelpiece.

'It just didn't seem a very good idea...' he said.

'Because you realised that you could have me and that, really, I wasn't your type? Could that be the reason?' Every word was fired with the precision of a gun aimed directly at herself. 'I was amusing when I was a challenge and when you thought that you had a bit of competition. Sleeping with me was something you did because, in your great wisdom, you decided that the competition in question wasn't of the right quality. Am I heading along the right lines here, Rocco? Am I working things out correctly? I guess if I hadn't delivered a blow to your masculine pride, you might have just left it there, but you had to sleep with me again, had to make sure that you could get me into bed, so that you could prove to yourself that my attraction to you hadn't been a one-off thing.'

And all those bits that she hadn't added. The bits about her and her motivations. The bits about the way she had tried to fight what she felt only to discover that it was bigger and stronger than all the defences she could erect.

Now it was her turn to feel her anger swell as he stood there by the mantelpiece in complete silence. The complete, telling silence, she thought, of agreement. A fresh wave of humiliation washed over her.

'I'd agree with every word of that if I could,' Rocco eventually said in such a low voice that Amy wasn't sure she had heard properly.

'I can't hear you!'

'I said,' he enunciated loudly, accusingly, 'that I would love nothing better to agree with you if I could.' He shook his head as if trying to clear it and glared at her. 'If I had had all that planned out the way you say, then at least I could tell myself that I was in control.'

'I…I don't know what you're trying to say…' Amy's eyes widened and she tried to grapple with the meaning of his words, but it was like trying to decipher a string of double Dutch.

'This is entirely your fault,' Rocco threw at her, stepping forward towards her and dragging a footstool over so that he was sitting right next to her but at a lower level. For once, *he* was looking up at *her*, although it still did nothing to calm her gut-wrenching tension.

'I might have expected you to blame me for everything.'

'I was absolutely fine and in control of every cornerstone of my life until you waltzed into it.'

'Which is exactly what could be said about me!' Amy burst out, without thinking, and Rocco looked at her, searching her face for answers.

'I mean...' she retreated in panic '...one minute we were all a happy little team, doing a job we loved, and then you come along and blow everything to pieces...'

'Everyone needs a shake-up now and again in their lives.'

'Or else what?' Amy queried waspishly. 'They might just explode from over-contentment?'

'What about Sam? Are you telling me that you were contented with that relationship?'

'No. If you want the truth, it wasn't going anywhere, but that doesn't mean that you had a right to try and get involved.'

'I had no choice.' Rocco looked down and linked his fingers behind his neck. It just wasn't fair that he could attack her and bring her to tears and still manage to do the vulnerability thing, Amy thought bitterly.

'Because someone was pointing a gun to your head?'

'Because...'

There was a deafening silence while he visibly sought to express himself and Amy found herself floundering in unknown waters. What was he trying to say? Whatever it was, it didn't make him feel very comfortable, judging from the rigid set of his shoulders and the cautious, defensive look he was now levelling on her.

'I didn't sleep with you...to prove a point. I let you think that and maybe I let myself think that as well. I slept with you because I was driven to.'

As declarations went, it was astounding enough to make her mouth fall open in sheer amazement.

Rocco gave a short, dry laugh devoid of any amusement.

'Why didn't you say that?' Amy whispered. Hope, resilient to the last, began slithering like a tenacious vine through the debris of her emotions.

'Because…because *driven*, except when it refers to work, has never been something I have experienced.'

Another tendril of hope shot through her but, like someone adrift on stormy waters, confronted with a slither of wood, she refused to cling to it.

'You have no idea what went through me when you told me that I had been nothing but someone there at the right time to take your mind off your recently departed lover.'

'He was never my lover,' she confirmed, hands balled into fists at her sides. 'He was my mistake. And I only threw that at you because I was retaliating at what *you* had told *me*.'

Something flickered in Rocco's eyes and he looked at her with piercing, savage intensity.

Amy sensed it and knew that if he was only aware of just how deeply her feelings for him ran, then he would make his move and she would be lost.

'I never said that I wasn't attracted to you…' she wavered. 'I thought that's why we were here…'

'It is why we are here,' Rocco grated. 'But I am not sure…'

'Okay.'

'No, it is emphatically *not* OK!' The harsh escalation of his voice brought Amy's head snapping up in shock. 'Correction, it might be *OK* for you…a bit of lust between the sheets, your first steps out of the cocoon you've been living in before you hit the big, bad world out there!'

'What are you talking about?'

'You know exactly what I am talking about! Look at you! As competent as any businesswoman I have ever met, and why do you think that is?' He didn't give her the opportunity to answer. He steamrollered any possible response before she had time to get a syllable out. 'Because you have given everything to your job. At sixteen, it was your escape and you were determined enough to climb every rung of the ladder, only focusing on what lay ahead. You threw everything you had into work and men were sidelined into entertainment when you thought you needed it. Which,' he added shrewdly, 'was probably not very often. And now, you are on the brink of a brave new world, you're willing to start flexing your sexuality and I don't intend to be your first stepping-stone.'

Flexing her sexuality? Amy wondered dazedly if they were talking about the same woman. *He didn't want to be her first stepping-stone?* As if she had suddenly turned into a predator of innocent young men and had dark intentions of gobbling them up one by one? She opened her mouth to try and point out the glaring misconception, but Rocco was on a roll.

'I never thought I would hear myself say this but...' He paused and shot her a look that was openly, heart-tuggingly, bemused.

'But...?' She leaned forward, heart racing, dreading further disappointment but unable to beat back the flood of hope. 'I'm not asking for commitment,' she forestalled anything that might be going in that direction.

'Which is my problem,' Rocco confessed with raw emotion. 'Why not?'

'You said...'

'I know what I said. And once I meant every word of it, but sleeping with you isn't enough. I want strings attached. In fact, I want so many strings that you're tied up completely.'

'You want strings…? Attached…?' A tremulous smile broke like sun peeping out from behind a bank of clouds.

'You find that amusing?'

'I find that…' she reached out and stroked the side of his face with a trembling hand and shuddered when he caught it with his and held it tightly '…I find that very…satisfying.'

'And why would that be?'

'Because I love you,' Amy replied simply. 'At first, I just wanted to get away from you because I knew that I couldn't love you and be with you without getting hurt, because I knew that you weren't looking for a relationship, but then…tonight…I didn't care any more about protecting myself. I just wanted you.'

Rocco gave a low-throated laugh and kissed her knuckles, then looked up at her from under his gloriously long lashes.

'Of course you did.' He pulled her down to him and they fell backwards on the carpet, untangling themselves with breathless laughter. He rolled her onto her side so that he could look at her. 'Even when you were still going out with that man, I bet you only had eyes for me.'

'How did you know?'

Rocco flipped her onto her back and covered her legs with one heavy thigh.

'Hoped, my darling. Hoped and wanted because it's impossible to believe you could ever have eyes for anyone else when you are the object of all the love I have in my heart.' He tenderly kissed the nape of her neck and murmured warmly into her ear. 'You know you have to marry me, don't you?'

'Have to…?'

'No choice, I'm afraid.'

'In that case…I'd be a fool to argue, then, wouldn't I…?'

Antonio looked at his son and the young woman who had been as close to him as his own daughter for so many years and was filled with the richness of contentment.

In his most secret dreams, he had never dared hope that he might be blessed with a reconciliation with his son. He had nursed his private regrets and accepted the distance between them with the weary resignation of an old man who had given up expecting the unexpected.

But reconciliation this most certainly was. In fact, the past week spent with his son and his daughter-in-law had been the happiest days of his life. So much catching up to do. To think that he had missed so much because of his ignorance and pride. To imagine that the bond he should have forged with his only son had been lost because, in his despair and grief, he had pushed the child away only to watch the child become a man and do the same to him. Serena had been taken from him, yes, but it had never been Rocco's fault and he had finally found the courage to tell him that, to tell him how his own misplaced pride had allowed barriers to be built between them that the years had further cemented.

Amy had mellowed him, he thought now, watching as they strolled back from their walk along the private beach, fingers loosely linked, their body language speaking volumes. He was relaxed, he laughed and when he looked at her there was such love in his eyes that Antonio almost felt he could reach out and capture some and bottle it.

He waved at them as they approached.

'You should have come walking with us, Antonio.' Amy smiled at him and gave him a quick hug. 'It's beautiful here.'

'A man could forget about the reason for working in a place like this.' Rocco looked at his father and grinned.

'And I know a man who has,' Antonio informed his son. 'Not that he would not appreciate a little company from foreign shores now and again…' One more week and they would be gone. He would miss them more than he could express. 'And, of course, whoever else might accompany them in due course…'

'Friends, you mean?' Amy asked innocently and Antonio and his son exchanged a wryly knowing look.

'Somewhat closer than that.' Rocco laughed, pulling her to him and kissing the top of her head, which smelt of sun and cool breezes. 'More along the lines of family, but little ones…'

'Well, we'll have to work on that,' Amy murmured softly, eyes shining at every dream she had ever had that had now come true.

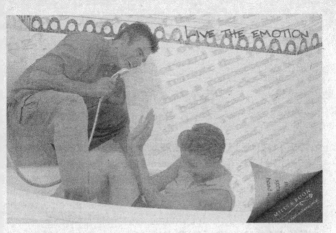

FREE

4 BOOKS AND A SURPRISE GIFT!

We would like to take this opportunity to thank you for reading this Mills & Boon® book by offering you the chance to take FOUR more specially selected titles from the Modern Romance™ series absolutely FREE! We're also making this offer to introduce you to the benefits of the Reader Service™—

- ★ **FREE home delivery**
- ★ **FREE gifts and competitions**
- ★ **FREE monthly Newsletter**
- ★ **Books available before they're in the shops**
- ★ **Exclusive Reader Service offers**

Accepting these FREE books and gift places you under no obligation to buy; you may cancel at any time, even after receiving your free shipment. Simply complete your details below and return the entire page to the address below. You don't even need a stamp!

YES! Please send me 4 free Modern Romance books and a surprise gift. I understand that unless you hear from me, I will receive 6 superb new titles every month for just £2.69 each, postage and packing free. I am under no obligation to purchase any books and may cancel my subscription at any time. The free books and gift will be mine to keep in any case.

P4ZEE

Ms/Mrs/Miss/Mr............................Initials ....

BLOCK CAPITALS PLEASE

Surname ....

Address ....

....

....Postcode ....

Send this whole page to:

The Reader Service, FREEPOST CN81, Croydon, CR9 3WZ

Offer valid in UK only and is not available to current Reader Service™subscribers to this series. Overseas and Eire please write for details. We reserve the right to refuse an application and applicants must be aged 18 years or over. Only one application per household. Terms and prices subject to change without notice. Offer expires 28th November 2004. As a result of this application, you may receive offers from Harlequin Mills & Boon and other carefully selected companies. If you would prefer not to share in this opportunity please write to The Data Manager at PO Box 676, Richmond, TW9 1WU.

Mills & Boon® is a registered trademark owned by Harlequin Mills & Boon Limited.
Modern Romance™ is being used as a trademark. The Reader Service™ is being used as a trademark.